"You know those pants I was wearing this morning?" George began slowly.

"The ones I dropped off at the cleaners on Columbus Avenue that's only open until five during the summer?" he continued.

It took a few seconds to sink in. And then Andie remembered with crystal clarity the set of keys to her apartment that had been hastily dropped into the pocket of the pants in question. "Oh, George!" she cried. "You *forgot?* The great George Demarest who types messages on red three-by-five index cards, and files junk mail in alphabetical order? *You forgot?*"

"Don't worry," he said briskly. "I'm sure they're still in my pocket. We'll pick them up tomorrow as soon as the place opens."

"Tomorrow?" Andie was aghast. "And where do you propose I sleep until then?"

George gave her a dazzling smile. "I assure you, Andie, your charms have not been showered upon me in vain." He paused, waiting for the power of his probing eyes to captivate her. "Tonight," he continued, as if bestowing a great favor, "you'll be sleeping with me."

Diana Morgan

Diana Morgan is a pseudonym for a husband-and-wife team who only moonlight as writers. By day they are two of New York's busiest literary agents. They met at a phone booth at Columbia University in 1977, and have been together romantically and professionally ever since.

"We began writing together strictly by accident," they confess, "deriving our pen name from our cat, Dinah Cat Morgenstern." Writing turned out to be a welcome form of comic relief from the pressures of business.

"This is a wonderful opportunity for us to talk directly to you, the reader. Our books have often been described as humorous or zany, but we feel there is an underlying seriousness to even our craziest story. What we hope to convey is a certain joie de vivre that will escape from the pages into a part of your life. Whenever we accomplish that, we feel like a million bucks. If we do, please write to us in care of SECOND CHANCE AT LOVE and let us know."

The Morgans enjoy opera, pigging out, small children, and elves (especially their daughter, Elizabeth), and trying to figure out what will happen next on *Hill Street Blues*.

Dear Reader:

April is a time of warm, wondrous renewal ... and, of course, heady romance. And Christa Merlin begins this month's list of SECOND CHANCE AT LOVE books with her most powerful story ever, *Snowflame* (#328). When Bruce McClure arrives at a mountain hunting lodge, he unexpectedly encounters beautiful Elaine Jeffrey, whose husband has recently been killed in a tragic shooting accident. Beneath Elaine's reserved politeness, Bruce senses her terrible anguish. He can't help offering the comfort he knows she craves ... or prevent passion from surging into sudden, overwhelming love. But he can't accept the agonized words she spills out: that her husband committed suicide — and she could have prevented it! Poignant and compelling, *Snowflame* is a love story that will captivate you from the very first page.

The main ingredient in Diana Morgan's latest romance is pure fun. Take one distraught soap opera writer, Andie Maguire, whose furniture has been abandoned on a New York City sidewalk. Add one handsome but harried efficiency expert, George Demarest, whose cousin has left him with a scruffy toddler. Make the tyke a terrible two-year-old called Speedy, whom Andie agrees to baby-sit — and you've got the zany confection, *Bringing Up Baby* (#329). Don't miss this irresistible romance of hilarious catastrophes and inventive charm.

In *Dillon's Promise* (#330), the ever imaginative Cinda Richards brings you the lovable, roguish, obstinate, utterly unforgettable Scotsman Dillon Cameron. Haunted by a deathbed promise, and shocked to learn that, in a moment of wrenching grief, he fathered a child by his best friend's American widow, Dillon storms Thea Kearney's cottage, intent on claiming "his lasses." But Thea and her baby daughter have little use for such a heartbreaking rover now. Drawing on Scots legends and the magic of the seaswept highlands, Cinda Richards weaves a tale rich in humor, poignancy, and romance.

Next, Hilary Cole returns with *Be Mine, Valentine* (#331), whose Cary Grant-like hero, eccentric supporting cast, and whimsical story line evoke the charm of several silver-screen classics. Heiress Melanie Carroway's unusual family — the butler drinks, and her aunt thinks the dog is her reincarnated lover — fails to prepare her for unconventional thief Peter Valentine. No *ordinary* burglar steals only kisses, gets hired to "protect" his victims, then proceeds to kidnap the boss's daughter! Witty, inventive, and downright funny, *Be Mine, Valentine* is a delightful tale from a writer whose skill is growing by leaps and bounds.

Rarely does a first novel blend lightness and intensity as masterfully as Kit Windham's *Southern Comfort* (#332). The story sounds deceptively simple — Kelly Winters reluctantly agrees to write the script for brash filmmaker Leo Myers's documentary on the Civil War, and travels with him to scout locations — but Kelly and Leo have an appealing complexity that makes for a lively, moving romance. As they dare to share the painful secrets of their pasts, they misunderstand each other in sad, funny, and very human ways that are guaranteed to endear them to every reader. Be one of the first to discover the work of talented Kit Windham, who's sure to be writing many more romances for SECOND CHANCE AT LOVE.

Though not new to readers of romance, Cassie Miles makes her debut at SECOND CHANCE AT LOVE with *No Place for a Lady* (#333), in which heroine Elaine Preston takes a giant step forward for womankind by becoming the first female professional football player. Her teammates remain skeptical, but not robust, insightful Curt Michaels, a former basketball ace who quite literally becomes her staunchest cheerleader! Elaine must go a long way before learning just where she "belongs" — on the field *and* in Curt's arms! — and every step provides thoroughly satisfying romantic entertainment.

With every warm wish that this month's SECOND CHANCE AT LOVE romances will bring a touch of magic into your life...

Ellen Edwards

Ellen Edwards, Senior Editor
SECOND CHANCE AT LOVE
The Berkley Publishing Group
200 Madison Avenue
New York, NY 10016

DIANA MORGAN
BRINGING UP BABY

A
SECOND CHANCE AT LOVE
BOOK

BRINGING UP BABY

First edition published April 1986

First printing

"Second Chance at Love" and the butterfly emblem are trademarks belonging to Jove Publications, Inc.

Printed in the United States of America

Second Chance at Love books are published by
The Berkley Publishing Group
200 Madison Avenue, New York, NY 10016

BRINGING UP BABY

Chapter One

"OKAY, LADY, THAT'LL be twenty bucks a floor extra to move ya in—that's per man."

Andie stood flabbergasted as the burly mover went back to working the wad of gum in his mouth. His three helpers all managed to look away, as if they had played this scene before. Here she was only an hour in New York City, and already she had a problem. Behind her was the brownstone she was about to make her new home, but it looked as if just getting her furniture inside was going to cost her a lot more than she had bargained for.

"I don't understand," she stalled, wiping her brow and pushing her sunglasses on top of her head. "When you left my home in Winston-Salem yesterday, you gave me a flat rate."

"Yeah, but that was before I knew you had rented a fourth-floor walkup," the man explained with a confident patience that Andie found somehow threatening. He was going to win, and he knew it.

She scowled. "New Yorkers," she drawled, deliberately letting her southern accent through. "If I had hired hometown boys, they would have kept their part of the bargain." She stared hard at the mover, but he didn't flinch. The only way to get her furniture up the three perilous flights of stairs was to pay this obnoxious fellow his outrageous fee. "Oh, all right," she said crossly. "Now, let's see. That's three flights times four men times twenty—"

"Four flights, lady." He pointed to the steps leading up to the front stoop, where two large stone gargoyles were sculptured on either side of the double oak doors. Andie wished the gargoyles would suddenly come alive and scare away these bandits, but she knew she would have to handle the situation herself.

"This is highway robbery," she protested, to no avail. Feeling cornered, she looked around desperately, as if expecting someone to materialize and help her confront the movers; but the only person who emerged from inside the building was a man with a thumb-sucking child in his arms.

He didn't even see her at first. Instead, he looked impatiently up the street, unconcerned with her dilemma. When at last he became cognizant of what was happening below him, he smiled politely.

"Moving in, I see," he surmised. His glance swept over her bluntly, his eyes taking in her windblown reddish hair, piquant face, and small but sturdy frame. They lingered on the skimpy T-shirt that said NORTH CAROLINA IS FOR LOVERS and dropped to the close-fitting faded jeans that covered her slender legs. It was a very cool once-over, but a once-over nonetheless, and Andie could tell from the approving glint in his eyes that he liked what he saw. She would have been unsettled by the open masculine interest that leaped from his eyes, but she was too busy observing their unique golden-brown color which matched his golden-brown hair. There was something dazzling about the combination that nearly took her breath away, as if he had been fashioned according to a very specific set of plans. He was of medium height, with a lean, powerful build, and his attractive physique was enhanced even more by the classically simple, immaculate way in which he was dressed. He looked like an ad in a magazine, only better; the perfection remained secondary to the vital sense of energy and masculine strength that pulsed underneath the polished exterior. Their eyes met, and a moment of recognition passed between them, of the kind that men and women have experienced for centuries, before the mover interrupted them.

"Okay, now," he began to calculate. "That's four flights with four men at twenty per man per flight."

"I suppose next you'll be counting how many steps to the fourth floor," Andie huffed.

"Fifty-three," the newcomer volunteered suddenly.

"What?" she asked, startled.

"Fifty-three steps to the top floor. And they'll have to lift that couch over the pointed finials at each landing. It's going to be quite a feat."

"Finials, huh?" The mover pondered. "I'd better go check that out." He bounded past her and inside the building.

Andie sighed angrily, but the man with the thumb-sucking toddler smiled. He stepped down so that he was on the same level with her, his smile sending a shaft of warmth running through her. His proximity was like a magnet, drawing her attention so strongly that she found herself unable to look away. And yet, despite his appeal, there was something almost comical about his demeanor. The child he was carrying presented a direct contrast to his elegant appearance; the little boy was dressed in baggy blue corduroy overalls, a blue-and-white striped shirt with stains on the collar, and small, grubby red sneakers. The man seemed unaware of the clash in styles, however; he even seemed oblivious to the fact that the child's grimy little hands were clasped around his crisp white collar. He looked as if he were about to chair an important business meeting, if only someone would remove the small person hanging around his neck. "I take it you're moving into the apartment above mine?" he asked.

"Yes, I'm Andie Maguire," she offered.

"George Demarest," he replied, extending a hand after getting a better grip on the child. "And this is Joshua Carmichael, otherwise known as Speedy."

Speedy looked at her with such disarming candor that she had to smile. He had a mop of brown hair and large blue eyes that didn't blink.

"I'm charmed," Andie said to him, gripping a tiny fist. She looked at George. "How old is he?"

"He's two. And I'm late for a very important business lunch," he added nervously. He glanced down the street and looked at his watch.

"Expecting someone?" she asked.

"Oh—uh, my cousin Mindy," he answered vaguely, looking at his watch again. "The kid's mother."

The little boy began to squirm, and George tightened his grip, letting out a heavy sigh. "She asked me to watch Speedy for her," he explained as he wrestled with the restless arms and legs. "She said she'd only be gone an hour."

Andie eyed him surreptitiously, wondering why on

earth he was taking care of this child at all. She still couldn't get over the contrast of this nearly perfect, devastatingly handsome man and the squirming toddler in his arms. "I'm sure your cousin will show up," she said.

"I'm not." He sighed. "That was three days ago."

Andie whipped around and stared at him. "Are you serious?"

He didn't answer, and she realized that he meant it. Yet he actually seemed to expect this cousin of his to arrive in the nick of time before his lunch date.

The burly mover reappeared. "Okay, lady," he said. "That'll be ten bucks per banister."

"Oh, great!" Andie exclaimed. She threw her new neighbor a pointed glare. "Thanks a lot."

"I'm terribly sorry," he said mechanically. He wasn't interested in her plight. He had problems of his own.

"Ain't his fault." The mover scratched his head and removed a pencil from behind his ear. "I'd have caught that the second we started movin' ya in. So let's see what this all comes to. Twenty times four times—" He mumbled to himself, nodding and scribbling until he arrived at a figure. "That'll be another three hundred and fifty— in advance."

Andie almost choked. "Three hundred and fifty!" With no one else to turn to, she appealed to George Demarest. "Do you believe these guys?" she asked. "They're trying to cheat me."

"Hey," the burly man protested. "I resent that insinuation. I gotta make a livin'. Maybe ya want me to leave all your stuff out here on the sidewalk?"

"You wouldn't dare."

"Oh, no? Okay, lady, you asked for it. Let's go, guys. Help me unload this stuff."

He marched back to his truck and actually began carrying out his threat. She watched, appalled, as he effortlessly dropped her coffee table right on the sidewalk next to a garbage pail. Next came her beloved armchair, followed by some bookshelves, followed by box upon box of records and dishes and odds and ends, followed by her potted palm tree, which they carelessly leaned against the railing. Each time they removed an article from the van, they had to pass by Andie. Her eyes sent daggers at them, but they stoically ignored her fury.

"What are you going to do after they leave?" George asked her curiously. His eyes were still searching around for his errant cousin.

Andie shrugged. "Necessity is the mother of invention. I'll think of something." She surveyed her belongings with a desperation that grew with every load the men dropped onto the street. "I can get those boxes inside by myself," she observed aloud, trying to sound confident.

"What about that heavy couch and those bookshelves?" George asked pointedly.

"And this desk, lady?" the mover interjected. "What're ya gonna do with this desk, huh?"

She looked at George, who shrugged. "He's got a point," he said.

Deflated, she had to agree. "I'd need a pack of mules to haul that up four flights of stairs."

"So what's it gonna be, lady?" the mover asked impatiently. "There ain't no mules around."

"No," she admitted. "There aren't any mules, but there are quite a few jackasses."

The burly man lost his temper. "That's it, lady. I don't need to stand here and be insulted." He turned to his men, who were hauling out the last of her cartons. "Get in the truck, we're leaving."

Without another word, the movers gathered their gear and, after closing up the doors of the truck, got in and prepared to leave.

"Your last chance, lady," the mover said, leaning aggressively out the window. Andie stood firm. It would be too humiliating to back down now. The driver gunned the engine as the truck sprang to life. "Bye-bye, lady. Welcome to New York."

The truck took off, leaving Andie to ponder her fate. She plunked down on the sofa, feeling hopelessly out of place sitting in the middle of the sidewalk. There was nothing to do but start working. She looked doubtfully at the mess on the sidewalk, where boxes were stacked perilously on top of one another. "Well, here goes nothing." She stood up bravely, rubbed her hands together, and tried to lift the first box, but she could barely hoist it off the ground. "Oooff," she grunted, dropping it back down. "I'm off to a great start."

"Ahemmmm." She glanced up and saw George Demarest looking down at her quizzically.

"What?" she asked suspiciously. He hadn't been any help at all so far. The last thing she needed was his unasked-for advice.

"May I offer a suggestion?"

"No," she answered flatly. "A strong back would be more useful."

She tried another box, this time managing to get it a few feet off the ground, but it was too heavy and she fell back onto the sofa, the box landing on top of her.

"You are persistent," George observed. "And stubborn."

"Stubborn? Me?"

"Yeah, like a mule." With Speedy hanging over his left arm, he easily lifted the box from her lap and placed it on the ground. "Mind if I join you?"

Andie sighed and gestured to the seat next to her. "There's plenty of room," she drawled.

George sat down and placed Speedy between them, eyeing her curiously. "My God," he said suddenly, "you *really* talk like that, don't you?"

Andie was confused. "What do you mean? Of course this is the way I talk." Her eyes narrowed. "You makin' fun of my accent, Yankee boy?"

"Yes," he said bluntly. "I've never heard anything quite like it. You sound like you're from central casting. I thought you were just putting on that southern-girl routine for those crooks so they'd take pity on you."

"That is not true," she said shortly and with dignity. Her southern accent was deep and feminine, but not sickly sweet. It curled around her words with a dry twist that revealed her strong sense of the absurd. She knew what phony feminine ploys sounded like, because she had heard them. And she knew *she* didn't sound that way—how could he accuse her of such a ridiculous strategy? She gave him a deeply suspicious look. "Are you here to insult me or help me?"

"To help you, of course."

"Then quit dawdling and pitch in."

He gave her a look to match the one she had just given him. "Hmmm," he said with an assessing glint in his eye. "You certainly are impatient. I suppose you're a reporter or magazine writer of some kind, aren't you?"

She became instantly defensive. "Why?"

"Because journalists work on tight schedules and always have deadlines. I have found them to be unduly impatient and easily prone to making quick—and often incorrect—decisions."

"Is that so?" She took a deep breath and stared at him,

finally nodding in resignation. "Well, I am a writer," she admitted reluctantly, ignoring his triumphant smile. "I'll be writing for a soap opera called *Until Tomorrow Comes*. I'm supposed to start work tomorrow morning. If I ever move in, that is. Now, are you going to start helping me or what?"

Suddenly, Speedy, who had been watching the pile of boxes with evident interest, scrambled off the couch and toddled over to the nearest pile, where he began tugging at the contents. George reached over and scooped him up again, depositing him back on the seat. Speedy looked around avidly and finally settled on Andie, giving her an irresistible grin.

"I like lady." Speedy beamed.

Andie smiled back at him. "I like you, too, honey," she said. "But right now—"

"I hungwy!" the little boy continued imperiously, tugging at her arm. "Jord, I hungwy!"

"Not now, Speedy," George mumbled.

"I wanna eat!" Speedy insisted, but George paid no attention.

"Now, here's how I see it," he began in businesslike tones.

"Eat now! Go eat!" Frustrated, the child abruptly stopped making demands and let out a series of wails that carried all the way up the block.

"He's hungry," Andie said gently, patting his head.

"And so am I, but first things first." George fished in his pocket and produced a small box of raisins, which Speedy immediately grabbed. The child stuffed his mouth with the raisins as George took a preliminary survey of Andie's entire stock of belongings.

"Hmmm, first we'll count the boxes." He made a quick count, rapidly calculating in his head. "Fifty-eight," he noted. "Let's see, we'll leave the couch for last, the coffee table is easy, and the lamps are a snap. That desk—" He shook his head and examined it. "Those finials will give us a small problem, but if we edge it sideways . . ." He mumbled to himself, his eyes squinting with another calculation. "No problem," he finished triumphantly.

Speedy continued to cram raisins into his small mouth, reaching into George's pocket when the supply was depleted. "No more," he informed them plaintively. "All gone."

"Hold your horses, Speedy," Andie said. "We'll be finished in a jiffy." Speedy looked dejected but was diverted once again by the intriguing boxes.

"So?" Andie asked. "What's the verdict?"

George looked at his watch. "My appointment is at one o'clock. We have to have you moved in no later than twelve-thirty, which is precisely sixty-seven minutes and forty seconds from now."

"Terrific," Andie said. "You've got it all figured out, but how are you going to accomplish it?"

George smiled engagingly. "I propose a contract. I get you moved in and you take care of Speedy for the afternoon. Do we have a deal?" His lambent eyes were disarmingly winsome.

"Maybe," she hedged. "It depends on what time you're coming back. I'm having drinks with my new boss at three o'clock."

George pondered for a moment. "Three o'clock, huh?" He seemed irritated that she was upsetting his perfect plan, and she swallowed back a grin. He was so utterly sure of himself that she couldn't imagine what would happen if someone actually said no to him. "I've got it," he announced smoothly. "Simply move your appointment to four, and we'll be fine."

Andie shook her head. "I can't do that," she said. "This is my first day. I'm not going to start out by moving appointments around."

"At the moment, I'd say you're in no position to bargain," he said sharply, apparently having given up the charm-and-disarm approach.

"Neither are you," she reminded him airily. "You need a baby-sitter, and I'm it. On my terms."

"Three o'clock," he mumbled, as if she had just made a shockingly impossible demand. He looked at his watch and contemplated. Then he looked up. "Does it matter where you have drinks?"

She frowned. "Not really."

"Great, then I have the solution. You simply invite your boss to have drinks at the same place I'm having lunch. Bring Speedy downtown to the restaurant at five to three and we'll switch off. It's a snap."

"I don't know," Andie said worriedly. "It sounds kind of iffy to me."

"How can you say that? It will be like clockwork."

The idea of clockwork was obviously appealing to him. She cast a glance at all her earthly possessions, and the sight of them sitting in the street was enough to make her agree to George's plan. But there was one obvious flaw. "Can I ask you one simple question?" she inquired. "How are you going to get all of this up those stairs in an hour? It would take at least ten men."

He chuckled broadly. "You leave that to me."

"All right," she said slowly. "But I still have to unpack."

"I'll help you with it later tonight," he offered promptly.

Andie lifted an eyebrow. "You know, George," she said, "you really should have gotten a baby-sitter. Then you wouldn't be in this mess."

He looked at her impatiently. "Don't you think I tried? I'm new at this game, you know."

"That's no excuse," Andie insisted. She gave him a long, candid look. "You're not very good at planning things, are you?" she asked after a long moment.

"What?"

"You should be more organized. That's your problem."

So his cool facade had a chink! "Me, not organized?" he repeated. "Are you serious?"

"You need a plan. Children really can't be counted on to stay on schedule. You have to be flexible."

"You don't know what you're talking about," he said heatedly. "I happen to pride myself on flexibility. But a child can change your life. Especially if you didn't plan on having him around for more than an hour."

Andie frowned. "You'll just have to reorganize your priorities and become more efficient. Learn to compromise between your time and Speedy's."

George was obviously swallowing his anger, because he leapt up suddenly, breathing hard, and leaned heavily against the railing of the steps. He almost kicked over a box marked FRAGILE, but managed to save it at the last minute, shaking his head in frustration. "I'm late for a million-dollar lunch appointment and you're giving me a lecture on child care—I don't believe this!"

Andie was unfazed. "You need a lecture," she said calmly. "First of all, Speedy is hungry. Second, he's getting tired. I can tell by the way he keeps rubbing his cheek. And third, you put his shoes on the wrong feet." She indicated Speedy's grubby sneakers, which pointed out in the wrong direction. "And finally, you should have called a baby-sitter way in advance of your business lunch."

George stared wildly at Speedy's shoes and muttered something unpleasant to himself.

Andie shook her head in disapproval. "Taking care of a child requires a lot of coordination," she informed him. "Just what do you do for a living, anyway?"

He sighed. "I'm a systems engineer." Noting her quizzical glance, he added resignedly, "An efficiency expert."

Andie burst out laughing. "Well, you certainly could have fooled me."

"I have a very successful business," George informed her stiffly. "At least I did until today. I must say, Ms. Maguire, your attitude is most unfair. In fact, it is downright irritating. I believe that if you carefully reconsider your position, you will find that you are sadly mistaken."

This dignified speech was interrupted by Speedy, whose round blue eyes grew wide with sudden importance. "I make pee!" he announced.

George took him on his lap. It was a foolish thing to do, but too late. He lifted Speedy up and examined the wet stain on his jeans.

"Oh, well," he said. "I was going to take these to the cleaners today anyway."

Andie looked at him sympathetically, then took the child and placed him next to her, being careful to seat him on an old newspaper. "I reiterate, he's tired and hungry. And now he needs a change."

George bit his lip and glanced at his watch. "Sixty-four minutes left. Look, do we have a deal or don't we?"

"Do I have a choice?"

"Do *I?*" George retorted.

"It's a deal," Andie said.

"Excellent," George concluded briskly, already eyeing the task in front of him as he transferred his gaze to the collection of her belongings.

Only instead of beginning the arduous task of moving her in, he settled back on the couch again.

"Well?" Andie asked after a long, weighty silence. "Shouldn't you get started?"

George smiled mysteriously. "I'm waiting for my help to arrive. They should be coming by here in precisely two minutes."

Andie didn't know what he was talking about. She was beginning to think he had conned her. "Two minutes, huh?" She frowned.

"Ninety-five seconds, to be exact." Suddenly, George's eyes lit up in satisfaction. "Ah, here they come now." He glanced quickly at his watch. "Eighty-nine seconds ahead of schedule."

Andie looked down the street. A group of about twelve high school boys in uniform was heading toward them.

"Hey, guys," George addressed them with congenial authority, "how'd you like to make a quick buck?" The boys stood together in a group, looking as if they always traveled in a pack. Andie wondered nervously if they were some kind of gang, like in *West Side Story*. They looked her up and down, silently assessing the situation. "A hundred and twenty dollars to move the lady in," George continued persuasively. "That's ten bucks a man."

The boys all exchanged glances and shrugged. They still hadn't spoken a word.

"A five-dollar bonus per man if you finish in an hour," George added. "A little incentive," he explained to Andie in an aside.

That did the trick. A short, fat boy in front of the group spoke for them. "Okay, guys," he said abruptly. "Let's do it." Andie watched, wide-eyed, as the group broke apart, their diffident attitude shattered. Bedlam set in as each one ran for a box, some lifting as many as three at a time. They were racing for the stairs when George stopped them.

"Hold it, hold it, everybody!" He waited as the boys stopped in confusion and turned. "Let's get coordinated. I want a bucket brigade set up."

They all stared at him darkly, reluctant to admit they didn't know what he was talking about. Andie hid a smile, careful not to wound their adolescent pride.

George explained rapidly. "Twelve boys divided by four flights of stairs. I want three guys on each level. You'll pass the boxes to one another without having to climb up and down each flight."

Comprehension dawned on the twelve stubborn faces. "Hey, man, that's cool," one of them remarked.

"Yeah," the short guy said. "I'll take the top level." He stretched out an upturned palm. "Keys, please."

Andie obligingly handed him her keys, and in a matter of minutes the boys were in position, three on each landing.

"Hey, lady!"

Andie craned her neck and saw the chubby kid's head leaning out of her window on the fourth floor.

"Here are your keys."

They fell haphazardly through the air, but George caught them easily, stuffing them into the pocket of his stained pants.

"Okay," he said, clicking a timer on his watch, "here we go."

Andie was impressed. One by one, George handed the boxes to the first man, who in turn handed them to the second—and so on, until the chain was working smoothly.

After a few boxes, George checked his watch. "It takes approximately twenty-three seconds for a box to travel to the top." He handed another box to the boy as he calculated in his head. "Let's see, five seconds per box times three per landing, subtract dropping a few, add in the fatigue factor..." He looked at Andie and smiled serenely. "Six minutes."

Andie didn't believe it. "It can't be done," she said.

But George ignored her skepticism and handed another box to the next available kid. "Why don't you change that diaper on Speedy?" he suggested casually. "I'm in Apartment 3-F, right below you." He dug into his pocket and handed her a set of keys. "You'll find everything you need in the old dumbwaiter."

Andie started to head inside with Speedy.

"Oh, and there's a TV dinner in the oven that will be just about ready."

"You feed this child TV dinners?"

"They're good enough for me," he said, adding, "and very efficient."

She turned away, shaking her head as a box was passed around her and up the stairs. "That man has a lot to learn," she announced to no one in particular.

"Oh, and Andie!"

She again turned slowly around to see him looking up at her.

"I took him down to Macy's yesterday and got him some clothes. You'll find clean overalls in the hall closet," he called up. "The diapers are in the old dumbwaiter on the wall. They work by an ingenious system of adhesive tabs. You don't have to worry about pins. It's really quite—"

"I know, I know," she said wearily. "Efficient, right?"

Chapter Two

ANDIE STOOD IN THE OPEN DOORWAY of George's apartment, awestruck. The place was dazzling, decorated entirely in white.

"This can't be for real," she breathed. Her hands automatically lifted her sunglasses from her eyes as if to correct a false impression, but that only made it worse.

"This isn't an apartment, it's an operating room," she said.

Speedy wriggled impatiently. "Eat now!" he demanded imperiously.

"In a second, honey. First I've got to adjust to the glare."

She walked into the living room, staring at the white walls, white furniture, white lamps, and a white area rug that was mercifully interwoven with a deep blue geometric design. The glass-topped coffee table gleamed in the sunlight, casting rays on the blue-and-white abstract wall hanging over the white couch. The opposite wall was completely mirrored, enhancing the illusion of light and space. Andie had to admit it was beautiful in its own way, immaculately clean and bright. Then she sighed. All in all, it was a spectacularly terrible place in which to house a rambunctious two-year-old.

She sat down gingerly on a white leather chair and looked around once more. "I know," she said to Speedy. "I've died and gone to heaven. That's the only explanation for all this."

Speedy ran aggressively over to a white floor lamp and began tugging at the cord. "Oh, no, you don't," she said, taking charge. She marched over and scooped him up in her arms. "Okay, kid, first we change you, the old-fashioned way. Now, where are those diapers?"

She poked around, finally discovering the dumbwaiter right next to the bathroom door. It was hidden by a crusty old door on ancient hinges, nearly camouflaged by several coats of gleaming white paint. The shelf inside held a neat stack of diapers, cotton balls, and containers of baby powder, arranged carefully between the tired old pulleys. She wondered idly if the dumbwaiter still worked and closed the door gingerly, latching it back into place.

A small mattress on the floor was obviously serving as a changing table, and she was gratified to see that it was tightly covered with a white sheet and a quilt, and adorned with a shabby teddy bear.

"Now, let's see if I remember how to do this." She recalled the years she had put in changing the diapers of her two younger brothers, and went to work. After placing Speedy on the mattress, she picked up the new diaper and positioned him on top of it. The old diaper came off, and her confidence renewed, she easily finished without mishap.

"There." She beamed after smoothing the tabs into place. "Good as new." She deposited the soiled diaper in a convenient nearby can and clapped her hands in triumph. "All in all, not a bad system for a bachelor. He really *is* quite efficient."

But Speedy wasn't going to let her get away that easily. In one well-placed sweep of a fist, he managed to kick the stack of diapers onto the floor. The cotton balls were next, quickly followed by the baby powder.

Andie hastened to stop him, but he only broke into a huge giggle.

"Oh, so you think it's funny, huh?"

"Go eat now?" he asked hopefully.

"All right, all right," she said. "You win. But you don't win fair."

Suddenly, a loud bell began to ring in the kitchen, making Andie jump in surprise. "Holy cow!" she exclaimed. "What in the name of—"

Before she could do anything about it, George burst in. "The TV dinner is ready," he announced, heading straight to the kitchen. He proceeded to go into a highly mechanical routine so precisely orchestrated that Andie didn't know whether to laugh or applaud. In one fell swoop, he silenced the alarm sitting on top of the refrigerator, retrieved the TV dinner from the oven, placed it in the freezer, and then reset the alarm clock.

"It will cool to the right temperature in two and a half minutes," he explained. "Now for the milk bottle." A flip of a knob on the gas stove and in no time at all a baby bottle filled with milk was warming in a pot of water.

"How many seconds for that?" Andie asked, a bit dubiously.

"Seventy to eighty-five," he answered promptly, casting her a glance that instantly silenced her. He obviously knew exactly what he was doing, and just as obviously intended to remain in control. His eyes lingered on her for a moment, taking in the sight of her startled, slightly flushed face. Then they lit with an inner amusement, as if he were simply waiting for her to acknowledge his brilliance. His absolute confidence simultaneously commanded her respect and irritated her.

He checked the timer on top of the refrigerator. "The alarm should go off about the same time the TV dinner is ready to come out of the freezer."

"Incredible," she mused. Testing him, she continued, "I'll bet you can even tell the exact time those kids will finish moving me in."

His eyes accepted the challenge easily, sweeping over her with a disturbing slowness. "They finished three minutes ago."

Andie's face almost fell, but George didn't stop to gloat. While she watched him with growing amazement, he sped into the bedroom, loosening his tie.

"I'll be right out," he called. "I just have to change." The door closed for approximately one and a half minutes. Andie waited curiously, somehow unsettled by the knowledge that George was undressing only a few feet away. The decidedly unladylike thought crossed her mind that she wouldn't mind watching him. He was so sleek and dapper on the outside that she longed to see the sinewy, masculine body she knew was underneath the impeccable surface.

Off went the alarm, and at the same instant out burst George, dressed in a dark blue suit. The stained pants he had been wearing before were draped over his arm, and he quickly hung them over the doorknob before grabbing a new tie.

Andie gulped, her eyes moving over his lithe, powerful form. "That was certainly fast."

His eyes locked with hers, and one eyebrow arched slightly. "Of course." He adjusted his tie as he strode past her into the kitchen to turn off the alarm. "Okay, let's take that dinner out of the freezer and get that kid fed."

Out came the dinner, the milk, and a bib. Before Andie could utter a word, George took three phone books down from a corner shelf and plopped them on a chair at the small table in the kitchen. Then he quickly transferred the food onto a plastic plate and cut everything into small pieces. Picking Speedy up, he deposited the child on the phone books, tied on the bib, and set the plastic plate in front of him. His movements had a rhythm and an energy of their own that were fascinating to watch. But they stopped abruptly when he spotted the diapers and cotton balls and spilled baby powder on the floor.

"What's this mess?" he asked critically.

Andie opened her mouth to explain, but George dismissed her explanation and took over, gathering up the scattered items and placing them neatly back on the shelf of the closet.

"Okay, let me set you straight on where I'm having lunch." He marched into his bedroom and Andie could hear the clicking of an electric typewriter. When he came out he handed her a red 3 x 5 index card, neatly typed with the name, address, and phone number of the restaurant.

"A red index card?" she asked quizzically. "What's wrong with a white one?"

"It's all psychological," he explained with appealing earnestness. "Industrial psychologists did a study on color and human response." He went back into his room to get something, raising his voice as he continued his monologue. "Red works best for appointments."

"But why did you type it?" she couldn't resist asking. She had the feeling that she didn't really want to know the answer, but something about his compelling manner intrigued her enough to pursue it. "A pencil or pen would have been fine," she added almost baitingly.

There was no answer.

"Uh, George?"

Out he came, carrying a half-open briefcase in his arms. After examining it to make sure the necessary papers were there, he closed it with a sure snap and placed it neatly by the door.

"Better call your boss and tell him to meet you there at three o'clock," he ordered.

She obeyed automatically, venturing into the bedroom. It was just like the living room, only more practical. Besides a captain's bed with drawers in it, there was an entire office set up. One corner was occupied by a computer and a printer. Next to that was a desk, gleaming and empty except for the phone, and a red index card like the one in her hand. It bore the name of George's lunch companion, typed in the exact center.

She picked up the phone and dialed the number of the studio. "This is Andie Maguire," she said brightly, anxious to make a good impression. "Is Mr. Collier in?" There was a pause before a disgruntled voice came on the line.

"Collier here, what is it now?"

"Well, hello there," Andie said, summoning enthusiasm into her voice. "It's me, Andie Maguire."

"Who?"

She blinked and ordered herself not to panic. She had

just moved her entire life to a strange city. "Uh, Andie Maguire," she repeated cautiously. "I'm your new writer—for *Until Tomorrow Comes.*"

"Terrific," he said, rustling some papers on his desk. "We can use some fresh blood around here. I just fired my head writer." He stopped suddenly and asked, "Oh, wait a second, are you that kid from South Carolina?"

"Uh, yes, sir—North Carolina, actually. Do you remember now? We had an interview in Raleigh last month."

"So, when can you start?" Collier barked.

"Well," she said hopefully, "I thought we'd meet for a drink and, uh,—"

"A drink?"

"Well, last time we talked you said we should meet for a drink before I started work."

"I did, huh?"

"Well—of course it doesn't have to be a drink," she floundered.

George's face appeared in the doorway, directing her with his innate confidence. "Yes, it does have to be a drink," he announced, pointing to the red card in her hand. "Remember our agreement?"

Andie gazed at the red card in consternation and took another shot at Collier.

"Yes, it does have to be a drink," she said automatically, biting back her surprise at her own boldness.

"Okay, that's fine by me." Collier was suddenly expansive, sounding almost amused. "After today's taping, I'll be needing a drink—a lot of them. I'll meet you, say at two-thirty, at the Museum Café on Columbus and Seventy-seventh. It's right down the street from the studio and—"

"No!" Andie said firmly.

"No? What do you mean, no?"

"I've got a better place to meet," she explained hurriedly.

Collier let out a sigh on his end while Andie gave George a pleading look. George took the red card from her hand and held it in front of her eyes. "'21' Club," she said coolly into the phone.

There was a long pause at the other end, followed by a huge guffaw. "'21' Club?"

"Yes," Andie answered bravely after her boss had stopped laughing. "I have the address right in front of me. It's at Twenty-one West Fifty-second Street."

"I know where it is," Collier said.

She stared at the card for a second, before adding, "Now, that's clever."

"Yeah, what is?"

"Naming a restaurant after the address."

"Yeah, brilliant," her boss agreed.

"And since you'll need more time to get there, we can meet at say—" She looked at George before answering, catching the clear calculation in his eyes. "Three o'clock."

There was a long silence. "Uh, Mr. Collier? Are you still there?"

"Yeah, I'm still here. Drinks, huh?"

"At the 21 Restaurant."

Again Collier began to chuckle. "Three o'clock," he repeated. "Okay, I'll see you at the '21 Restaurant' at three." He hung up, still chuckling, and Andie smiled uneasily as she looked at George.

"So?" he asked. "Are we set?"

"I don't know about this, George."

He led her back into the living room, his hand resting lightly on the small of her back. His nearness was as commanding as his authoritative attitude, almost crackling with masculine control. "What's to know? Just show up with Speedy at three outside the '21' Club, and I'll take him off your hands. What could possibly go wrong?"

"Everything," she said darkly.

He gave her a disarming smile that made her pulse jump. "Look, I'll set the alarm on my watch for three, okay?" He meticulously set a tiny dial and marched over to the white sofa.

"Now for Speedy's bed." Picking up the cushions, he deftly pulled out the bed and lined up the cushions on both sides of the mattress. "This is so the little bandit doesn't fall off," he explained. "His blanket," he continued, producing a blue wool blanket from underneath the sofa, "and his pillow. *Voilà!*"

Andie nodded, impressed. "I must admit, you do have a system."

"Of course," he said graciously, accepting her praise as if it were long overdue. "I *am* an efficiency expert, you know." His eyes sparkled as he caught her glance, and she could tell that he was suppressing his amusement. Draping the stained pants over one arm and picking up his briefcase with the other, he opened the door with aplomb. She had never seen anyone so effortlessly in charge of a situation, and suddenly she wasn't so sure he had her best interests in mind.

"Hey, George," she said suspiciously.

He stopped for a moment and then turned with crushing poise.

"Three o'clock. On the dot. Don't forget, now."

He smiled condescendingly and walked back, standing only inches in front of her. His closeness was unsettling, not because he was really threatening but because he was so very solid and appealing.

Something deep within her stirred. An uncanny feminine instinct told her that he wasn't going to be just her friend and he wasn't going to be merely her neighbor. The spark between them was fanning into flame, and she was positive that he felt the sudden change as strongly as she did. For a long moment, their eyes locked and Andie struggled to look unruffled.

"Why don't we make that five to three," George suggested finally. "You'll need the extra five minutes to tidy up. After all, you'll be meeting with your new boss after taking care of a two-year-old. You just may look a mess." His eyes swept candidly over her trim frame, taking in the faded jeans, ancient sneakers, and ragged T-shirt. His words indicated that he was talking about her clothes, but his eyes seemed to bore right through the modest garments to focus on what was underneath.

Andie's face dropped. "Uh—maybe you're right," she conceded lamely.

"Of course." He marched off with a definite air of victory, and Andie felt a distinct sense of relief. But just as he reached the door, he turned back once again.

"Yes?" she asked, holding on to her cool facade.

"I had those kids hang all your dresses in the front closet before they left. Wear the red dress with the V neck." There was a wicked glint in his extraordinary eyes.

Andie was taken aback but answered readily, "I thought I'd wear the black suit. It's more businesslike."

"It is," he agreed as the door started to close behind him, "but I'm curious to see what you look like in that dress."

She could have sworn that he actually winked at her before shutting the door.

Andie had little time to ponder George's motives. As she turned away from the door, she saw that Speedy had somehow managed to empty his entire plate. Unfortunately, not all of the food had gone into his mouth. At least half of it had been mashed into pulpy tidbits and then thrown pell-mell onto the floor. Horrified, she dashed over and went to work with paper towels, finishing by scrubbing away at Speedy's plump cheeks.

"Now I know why they nicknamed you Speedy," she muttered as she removed the last of the evidence and placed the dish in the sink.

"Sleep now?" Speedy asked, looking up at her innocently.

"Excellent idea," Andie agreed, wondering how a half hour had gone by so quickly. "You're going to go to sleep right now. And then I'm going to take a bath and get out of these clothes."

An hour and a half later, Andie was still waiting for Speedy to wake up. She had managed a shower in George's awesomely clean bathroom with no trouble, and had wrapped herself in an oversized terry-cloth bathrobe. Her reddish hair had dried naturally in free-flying waves, and she had used the cosmetics that she carried in her purse. Now it was almost two-thirty, and she didn't know what to do. It wasn't a great idea to awaken a sleeping child, but necessity was beginning to demand it. She still hadn't gone up to her apartment to get her clothes, and time was running short.

"Sorry, Speedy, old boy, but you're going to have to wake up now. Come on." She stroked his downy head tenderly, and a split-second later the child was sitting upright and smiling as though he had never been asleep at all.

"Go outside now?" he chirped.

"Well!" Andie exclaimed. "You certainly wake up fast."

"Go outside?"

"Okay, okay, we'll go outside, but first we've got to go upstairs to my new apartment, which I still haven't seen yet, and I've got to get dressed."

After changing Speedy, Andie shepherded him out the door and climbed the stairs to her own apartment. But when she got there, her heart dropped. "Oh, no!" she cried aloud. "George still has my keys!"

A wave of dismay shot through her as she realized what this meant. Running back down the stairs with Speedy balanced on one hip, she burst into George's apartment and made a mad dash for a phone.

"Hello, Information . . . is this Information? I need the number of Restaurant 21—yes, yes, that's it, the '21' Club."

She punched the buttons with shaking fingers. A man answered in haughty tones.

"'21' Club."

"George Demarest, please. He's—"

"Who?" The voice became slightly less haughty and definitely more rude.

"He's a patron there. He's having lunch with"—her eyes glanced at the red card on George's desk—"Mr. Jeremy Shere, chairman of the board of the General Dynamics Corporation." She gulped when she realized that this client of George's was a very big deal. Good Lord, she realized guiltily, George certainly had a right to be worried about this lunch date.

"I hungwy again," Speedy announced loudly. "Want choc-vit."

"Not now, sweetheart," she whispered hurriedly, adding into the phone, "Could you find him, please? It's very important."

There was a pause. "Just a moment, please, madam," the voice intoned. "I'll see what I can do."

"I want choc-vit!" Speedy persisted angrily. "Go get choc-vit, okay? I *need* it."

Andie was already frantic, and the man was taking forever. Finally, after several tedious minutes during which Speedy continued to nag her about the "choc-vit", the man came back on the phone.

"I'm sorry, madam, but I have strict orders that Mr. Demarest does not wish to be disturbed."

"But you don't understand! He promised to take the baby, and—" Andie stopped, realizing that she wasn't making sense. "All right," she said desperately. "Could I leave a message for him?" She didn't wait for a reply. "Tell him that I'm coming over there, with Speedy, right now. That I have no clothes and—"

"I beg your pardon?" the man interrupted.

"You heard me, I have no clothes and I'm coming down, right now."

"Madam," the man said nervously, "there's no need to come. I'll be more than happy to convey this message to him immediately."

"Oh, you will, will you?" Andie was suddenly furious. "Well, be sure to tell him that the baby is his responsibility now."

"Uh, yes, ma'am. But surely—"

Andie hung up the phone, too aggravated to care about her uncharacteristic rudeness.

"Get choc-vit now?" Speedy asked, the moment she was off the phone.

Andie smiled wickedly. "Yes, honey," she said. "I'm sure they have something chocolate on the menu over at that 21 place. Let's get going."

The taxi driver had trouble pulling up directly in front of the "21" Club because of all the limousines and fancy cars that were double-parked in the street in front of it. Chauffeurs lingered importantly as they waited for their employers to emerge, but Andie was in no mood for ogling. She paid the driver just as a uniformed man appeared and opened the door. He looked surprised at the sight of Andie in her jeans and raggedy T-shirt, and he was clearly astonished when she calmly handed him Speedy. He took the child haplessly and waited for Andie to climb out before depositing him back in her arms.

The moment Andie had Speedy in her arms, she made a beeline for the door of the restaurant. The doorman ran after her but didn't catch her, managing to reach her only after she was already inside. She barely noticed all the stares as she entered the obviously sophisticated and exclusive inner sanctum of "21."

The nattily attired men and women at the bar were all aghast at the sight of the young woman who now stood in the main room of the restaurant with a toddler in her arms. And Speedy was not at all cooperative, sensing Andie's distress and fidgeting wildly as she looked around the dining room for George Demarest.

"I'm sorry, ma'am," the maître d' said as he approached her, "but you'll have to leave immediately." He took her arm firmly, and her grip on Speedy loosened.

"Ooooh," Speedy cried as he spied a tray of food balanced on a passing waiter's upturned palm. "I hungwy now. I eat!"

In the next instant, Speedy wriggled free and took off

in the direction of the waiter, his chubby legs propelling him, with Andie and the maître d' in hot pursuit.

They caught up with him halfway to a table where two very well-dressed men and a woman were dining.

"Up you go, kid," Andie said as she scooped him up, oblivious of the surprised diners. She gave them all a polite smile and then froze as she recognized them one by one. "Oh, my gosh," she gulped, backing away uneasily.

Staring back at her with bemused smiles were Mia Farrow, Andy Warhol, and Steven Spielberg.

A hand closed around her arm once more, but this time it did not belong to the maître d'. Andie looked up into the blazing eyes of George Demarest.

"Oh, good," she said shortly. "I found you. Here, take the baby. After all, he's your responsibility now."

"Lower your voice," George commanded as he tried to corner her off to one side, but Andie was not about to budge.

"I'm ruined," she wailed. "Look at me! I can't face my new boss looking like this."

"Why didn't you change?" he hissed angrily.

Her temper flared, replacing her panic. "Because *you* took your pants with my keys in them to the dry cleaners, that's why, Mr. Efficiency Expert!"

George blanched, and by now all the patrons had become wildly interested in this personal drama unfolding in the middle of the restaurant. The maître d' tried once more to subtlely remove them, but that was impossible.

"Please, Mr. Demarest," he pleaded. But Andie wouldn't let up.

"You locked me out of my own apartment, you fool!"

"All right, all right," George huffed. "I forgot all

about that, we were so short on time. I'm not used to rushing like that. If you hadn't bungled everything with those movers—"

"If *I* hadn't—"

"Look," George said imperiously, trying to take her arm. "I don't want to stand here arguing in the middle of the '21' Club."

"Thank you," the maître d' gushed. "Couldn't you both—"

"No," she snapped. "It's almost three o'clock. I've got an appointment in less than fifteen minutes with my new boss. What do you think he'll say when he sees me like this?"

George's eyes were sparkling with a new idea. "Fifteen minutes?" he repeated. "Listen to me. Now you'll see why I'm an efficiency expert. You'll go out now and buy a dress."

Andie stared at him furiously. "Are you crazy? In fifteen minutes?"

"Twenty," he countered. "You can be five minutes late," he reasoned, lifting Speedy and placing the child squarely on his shoulders. "Here's my charge card. Consider this my treat. Bergdorf's is only six minutes from here on Fifty-seventh and Fifth Avenue. Buy the first dress you see. Put in on there and hightail it back here. You can do it in under twenty minutes if you hurry. Now go."

"It can't be done," Andie protested.

"You're losing valuable time," George said as he pressed the timer on his watch. "You've already lost fifteen seconds."

"But—but—"

"Twenty seconds," he continued, unruffled. "Twenty-one, twenty-two, twenty-three..."

Chapter Three

SHE HAD NO CHOICE, really. She gazed at him wildly and then burst out the door. She felt as if she were in some kind of insane race, but she had recklessly decided to do this, and now she had to make it work. "Six minutes to Bergdorf's, huh?" she muttered as she jogged down the avenue. "Now he's an expert in time travel."

But sure enough, exactly six minutes later she was heading into Bergdorf Goodman with George's charge card still in her hand, storming through the cosmetics department toward an elevator. She got off at the first floor that sold dresses and the first thing she saw was a sleek mannequin elegantly clad in a deep blue square-cut dress with large front buttons and dolman sleeves. The straight skirt had pleats a third of the way down. It wasn't the sort of dress she usually wore, but it was stylish and she had no time to look any further. "I'll take that in a size eight," she informed the first saleswoman she found. "Just hold it for me and I'll be right back. Can you tell me where the shoe department is?"

"Which one?" the woman asked, fingering the pencil that was wedged over her ear. "Let's see, we have junior shoes on six, designer shoes next to Miss Bergdorf on eight, and—"

"The closest," Andie pleaded. "Quick."

The saleslady was thrown off-balance by Andie's excessive need for haste. "Oh, well, uh—let's see, uh—"

"Hurry!" Andie commanded.

"Uh, Plaza Two, just across the floor and to your left," came the puzzled response.

Andie was off and running.

"Will this be cash or—"

"Charge," Andie called out after her. "I'll bring the shoes back over here and you can write up the entire sale." She raced off in the direction of the nearest shoe department, nervously glancing at her watch every fifteen seconds. In no time at all, she managed to pick out a simple pair of blue pumps in her size, praying they would fit. She didn't have time to buy a pair of stockings, but Collier probably wouldn't notice.

"Four and a half minutes left," she muttered, realizing uncomfortably that she was getting more like George Demarest by the second. She grabbed the shoebox and ran back to the dress department. "Please," she begged the woman, "I've only got four minutes. Here's my charge card, start writing."

Without any questions, the saleslady went to work, taking only enough time to point out the direction of the dressing room.

"No time to lose," Andie reminded herself, jamming the dress and the shoebox under one arm as she ran for the nearest dressing room, tearing off the tags as she went.

Inside, she hastily climbed out of her jeans and T-shirt, tore off her sneakers, and stepped into the dress. It slid comfortably over her hips, and Andie breathed a sigh of relief. Thank goodness for the loose square cut. Sliding her feet into the shoes, she dared to step back and take a look at herself.

She looked decent. No, better than decent. She actually looked good. It was a much more sophisticated dress than she usually wore, but now that she had it on, she liked it.

She looked at her watch and saw that it was two minutes to three. Thank God her handbag was presentable, was her last coherent thought as she raced out of the dressing room and over to the counter where the saleslady had the sale written up.

"Here you go, Mrs. Demarest," she said, giving Andie a jolt.

"What!? Oh, but I'm not—" She bit back the rest of the sentence. "Thank you," Andie managed to choke out, reaching for the pen. Unfortunately, she then lost a precious ten seconds as she stared dumbstruck at the total amount. "Two hundred and ninety-nine dollars for the dress?" she whispered, stunned. "And a hundred fifty for the shoes?"

"Is there anything wrong, Mrs. Demarest?"

"Wrong? Uh—why, no." With a deep breath and a reckless shrug, she signed the receipt as Mrs. Andie Demarest. "He'll probably kill me for spending so much," she said aloud.

"Don't worry," the saleswoman responded. "Just take him out for a lovely dinner and let him see you in that dress before you tell him the price. You look beautiful, dear, simply radiant."

"Thank you," Andie said breathlessly.

A minute later, she found herself sprinting all the way

back to the restaurant, the new shoes pinching her feet as she ran. "Ah, good afternoon, madam," the maître d' said dryly as he consulted his appointment list. "You are . . . ?"

"Andie Demarest. No! I mean, Andie Maguire," she corrected herself, horrified at her mistake. "I'm meeting a Mr. Collier."

The maître d' found the name in his book and actually threw her a glance of minimal approval. "This way," he said. "Mr. Collier hasn't arrived yet. Would you like me to escort you to your seat?"

"He . . . hasn't arrived yet? You mean he's late? After all I went through?" She almost burst out laughing, but she threw back her head and gathered all of her poise together as she followed the maître d' through the glittering room. At that interesting moment, she caught sight of George. He was seated at a corner table with an elderly man. And perched on the old gentleman's lap, busily engaged in devouring a cup of chocolate mousse, was Speedy.

George looked up as she passed and his face registered instant approval. And not just approval, she couldn't help noticing. The man was impressed. Definitely impressed with the self-assured vision who waltzed majestically past his table. He pointed surreptitiously at his watch with a conspiratorial wink. "Twenty minutes exactly," he mouthed to her. "I told you so."

His lunch companion turned, and it was obvious from his look that he was equally impressed with the poised and stylish young woman in front of him.

George hastened to introduce her. "Oh, uh, Mr. Shere, this is Andie Maguire."

Andie shook his hand, trying not to disturb the little boy on his lap.

"Pudding," Speedy announced blissfully, chocolate smeared all over his mouth.

"Well, I can see you two have things well in hand," she

said graciously. "Now, if you'll both excuse me, I have an appointment." She reached out to shake George's hand and slipped him the receipt from Bergdorf's. "Take care."

George took the receipt and smiled. "It was my pleasure," he announced grandly without looking at it. His keen eyes followed her as she crossed the rest of the room, turning a few more heads as she followed the maître d' to a centrally placed table. She sat down regally and had just enough time to take one deep, steadying breath before Lou Collier was shown to the table.

"So you're the new kid on the block?" the gruff voice asked.

She looked up and saw a large, balding man wearing baggy trousers, a white shirt with the sleeves rolled up, and a wide tie that had gone out of fashion a few years before. His suit jacket was crumpled carelessly over one arm, and he flung it over the back of his chair before sitting down heavily.

"I'm Andie Maguire," she said, holding out her hand. "I'm delighted to meet you again."

"Yeah, I remember you now," he said, squinting at her and shaking her hand. "I'll have a Scotch on the rocks," he said to the waiter. "Make it a double." He turned back to Andie. "Hope I didn't keep you waiting," he apologized. "Things at the studio were insane today. I didn't think I'd make it out alive." He glanced at his watch. "Geez, I'm late, kid. Sorry about that. Well, at least *you're* prompt. I like that in a writer. Good habit to have."

"Thank you," Andie said, smiling serenely. He should only know, she thought as she calmly ordered a white wine spritzer. She took a long, slow breath and suddenly caught sight of George, who was watching her from across the room. He lifted a glass as if in a toast, and she gave him a tiny smile before turning back to her new boss.

* * *

"This way, ma'am, Mr. Demarest is waiting for you." The doorman gestured to a sleek black limousine that was parked ostentatiously in front of the "21" Club and escorted Andie over to its imposing depths.

Andie hesitated, squinting in the late afternoon sun. "No, I'm afraid you have the wrong person," she protested. "That's not my limo—"

The door opened unceremoniously, and George Demarest's head popped out. "Hi, Andie," he said cheerfully. His hand appeared from inside the luxurious vehicle, offering her a glass of champagne. "Come on in," he added hospitably.

"What's going on now?" she asked blankly.

A second later a small face completely covered with chocolate appeared. "I got choc-vit, Andie!" he announced proudly. In one grimy fist was a half-melted Hershey bar, and in the other was a gooey candy cane.

"Oh, Speedy," Andie said, forgetting everything else. "You are a mess."

"More choc-vit," he tried to say, but his words were garbled as he continued to stuff his tiny mouth.

Andie shook her head and reached in her purse for a tissue. Over the little boy's protests, she carefully and firmly wiped the mess from his chubby face. "Little children should not eat so much candy," she said to George. "You'll spoil him."

But George wasn't daunted. "We're celebrating," he informed her. "Come on in. I saved you some caviar."

Curious despite her disapproval, Andie climbed inside the spacious limo and looked around. The air-conditioning was a sudden and blessed relief from the sultry summer air of the city. She leaned back against the plush maroon seat and stretched luxuriously. To George's right was a compact bar, where he deposited the champagne bottle in an ice bucket. Directly in front was a TV set, which was tuned to *Sesame Street*, obviously for Speedy's entertainment. It seemed to be doing the trick, because Speedy was silently munching while his eyes were glued to the set.

George reached over and closed the door, effectively shutting out all the tireless outside noises of the city. Suddenly, the view was deliberately clouded by the gray-tinted windows of the limo, and Andie sank back in total surrender.

"This is heaven," she confessed. "You certainly travel first class."

George clinked his glass against hers. "Here's to you," he proposed smoothly. "For helping me make the biggest sale of my life."

"Who, me?"

"You and Speedy both," he admitted. "When old Jeremy Shere saw me walk back to his table with Speedy in my arms, his usually hard-driving corporate mask just about dissolved all over the table. Speedy brought out the grandfather in him."

"Yes, I could see that."

"You didn't see him sign my contract, did you?"

"Sorry, I must have been busy at the time."

George laughed. "He overheard our entire unfortunate conversation when you first walked in. When he saw you take off to buy the dress, he made me a promise right there. If you got back in the time I had allotted, he'd take me on as a consultant—for his entire company."

Andie's mouth fell open. "So you two were betting on me, is that it?"

He nodded smugly. "And you made it, right under the wire." George gave her a little pat on the hand that was probably meant to be friendly, but the look in his eyes was

anything but fraternal and his hand rested for a long, provocative moment on hers before he took it away. Her heart
jumped as she perceived his masculine interest. "I'm proud
of you, Andie," he said huskily. "You saved the day for
me—twice. Old man Shere was so impressed, he even
gave me the use of his limo for the day." His clinical
eyes softened, turning to a tantalizing sherry color. "Not
bad for a day's work, huh?"

"Not bad at all," she conceded, her voice lilting in
agreement. But she was determined to maintain some sense
of propriety. They had only just met, after all, and Speedy
was perched right next to them. "But I think," she added
carefully, "that it's time to go home now. We've all had a
very busy day, and Speedy needs to eat something besides
candy."

George looked disappointed. "What's the hurry? We've
got the limo for the rest of the day and evening." His eyes
sparkled with invitation. "I thought we could take a nice
long drive through the park. I could give you a grand tour
of the city."

Andie hesitated. The thought of cruising around town
with George in a limo was extremely tempting, but she was
exhausted from the day's events, and Speedy had been
dragged around for hours for their convenience. He needed
a bath and a square meal. "I'm sorry, George," she said
reluctantly, her eyes growing wistful for a moment. "Maybe
another time."

George drew back impatiently. She could see that he
wasn't used to being refused, and she hid a smile. Maybe
an occasional refusal would be good for him.

"What's the problem?" he asked.

She pointed at Speedy. "He needs a change and a bath.
I'm exhausted and I still have a lot to do. I never really had
lunch, and if I drink too much champagne on an empty

stomach, I may just collapse in your arms, a damsel in distress." The idea amused her, because she had the distinct feeling that George would savor the idea of rescuing her. But she didn't need to be rescued. It was time to get back to reality. She leaned forward and knocked on the partition.

"Yes, ma'am?" the driver's voice asked into a mike.

"Home, James," she said loftily, and then broke into a giggle.

"Columbus and Eighty-first," George added resignedly, and the massive car glided off.

"So," he asked evenly, "how did *your* meeting go?"

Andie laughed. "My boss is unbelievable. He's the exact opposite of you."

"Oh, really?" George asked coolly. "In what way?"

The urge to tease him rose up within her, and she decided to take advantage of it. George's controlled exterior begged to be challenged, and she ran her tongue lightly around her lips as she considered his question. "Well, for one thing he's an untypical dresser," she began. "Unless 1960's styles ever come back in. He's also very abrupt. His office is probably a mess." She turned and gave him a mischievous smile. "Very disorganized."

George lifted an eyebrow. "As opposed to me."

"No one is opposed to you, George. Or even in your league at all," she added, widening her green eyes deliberately. "You're unique. One of a kind. Totally different."

"Oh. Is that good?"

"I'm not sure," she hedged, giving him a long, impish sidelong glance. "I'll just have to find out for myself." She favored him with a tiny grin. "And I'm *sure* I'll find everything in its proper place."

For once, George seemed at a loss for words, but she wasn't getting the rise out of him that she had expected. He actually seemed to be enjoying her impromptu teasing.

It wasn't like her to flirt so audaciously, but she couldn't help it. There was something about George that brought it out in her. He was so perfect, so controlled, so utterly sure of himself and his world that a feminine demon in her longed to topple the marble god from his pedestal. A deeply rooted part of her wanted to see him vulnerable—not out of weakness, but out of passion. For her.

"You know," the demon continued, shaking her hair around her face, "I think sometimes this organization of yours actually works against you."

This appeared to be too much for him. He sat up and looked at her as if she were crazy. "Are you serious? How could it possibly work against me?"

"You see?" she persisted. "You can't even imagine a situation in which you might be wrong, can you?"

"No," George answered stonily. "I have found that my lifestyle works at peak efficiency for me."

"Really," Andie drawled, her eyes narrowing gracefully. "I'll bet you can't think of anything that can't be planned, filed, organized, cataloged, or timed. Can you?" she prodded.

"No, I can't," he said crossly. "There is nothing wrong with being organized."

Aha! So she was going to get a rise out of him after all. "No, there isn't," she agreed. "But you go beyond that."

"Give me one example," he challenged, the gleam that had sparked his eyes turning hard.

Andie pointed a playful finger at him. "Okay, I will. You file unsolicited mail."

"So?"

She almost lost her cool. "You don't think there's anything strange about filing mail that was addressed to Occupant—in alphabetical order?" She looked at him oddly. "What do you do with that stuff, anyway?"

"I think I should ask you what you were doing snooping in my files."

"I wasn't snooping, I was looking for a sponge."

George nearly choked on his champagne. "In my files? Why would I put a sponge in my files?"

"I'm sorry I looked," she apologized, looking down to hide her smile, "but I couldn't resist. I never saw such a place in my life. Every object in your apartment seems to have been put there with incredible forethought. Your shoes are in three rows by two deep, your shirts all hang facing the same way, your pants are perfectly hung exactly one inch apart. How did you get them spaced so evenly, anyway?"

He held up his thumb. "One inch, from joint to tip. And that's a professional secret. People pay money for that information, you know."

She swallowed champagne and stared at him in awe. "You are an amazing person, George Demarest."

"Thank you," he said, undaunted.

For once she couldn't think of a thing to say. The man was incredible, and he knew it. "I'm not asking you to live that way," he said. "But then again, I wasn't the one stuck with all my belongings out on the sidewalk this morning."

So now he was going to bait her, using the intractable tool of logic. Andie sighed. George seemed quite implacable. There was just no way to get to him, feminine wiles included. Too bad he's so damn good-looking, she thought grumpily, sneaking a look at his energetic profile. He's just too perfect for his own good.

George caught her sly glance and smiled enigmatically. "Don't sulk," he admonished. "It's so unbecoming. Especially on a woman as intriguing as you."

Her defenses stripped, she was barely able to do more than gape in surprise.

His hand reached for her arm, stroking it lightly. "Let's not play games, Andie. You are a very attractive woman, and a very clever one as well." He said nothing more, but his hand moved sinuously up and down her arm. A bolt of arousal swept through her, all the more powerful because she was so utterly unprepared for it.

"I'd like to kiss you right here," he murmured, his eyes raking over her. He inclined his head, indicating Speedy, who was still glued to *Sesame Street*. "And I'm not even sure he'd notice."

Andie's heart slammed against her chest. She had teased him to just this end, but now that he had taken her up on it, she felt totally unprepared. George was no first date to be "handled." He was a dynamic, mature man, ready and willing to take control of everything— including her.

His eyes were assessing her slowly. "But I don't think I will," he concluded, taking a sip of champagne. "Not yet."

Andie found her voice. "You certainly won't," she said. "Good heavens, George, we've only just met."

"True." His eyes sparkled. "But we've been through enough together since then to make up for the brevity of our acquaintance. You can't deny it, Andie. Fate threw us together, and I plan to keep us that way until I find out why."

His assurance was appalling, but it was also fascinating. "Oh, really?" she gasped.

"I won't rush you," he promised. A new twinkle stole into his eyes. "And it makes what I have to tell you a little easier."

Her heart lurched. "What?"

His hand resumed its sensuous journey up her arm.

"Well, I have some good news and some bad news for you."

Oh, no, she thought, what next? "Is that so?" she asked weakly.

"Bad news first," he decided. "I'm afraid there's been an unfortunate mistake."

"Well, out with it," she said. "Don't keep me in suspense."

He looked at his champagne glass and took a sip, seeming to weigh his next words carefully. "Come to think of it, it may not be bad news. It depends on your point of view."

Andie had no idea what he was getting at, and she couldn't imagine what sort of news he had that could possibly concern her.

"You know those pants I was wearing this morning?" he began slowly. She nodded. "The ones I dropped off at the cleaners before I went to my meeting?" Again he paused, waiting for her affirmative nod. "The cleaners on Columbus Avenue that's only open until five Monday through Thursday during the summer?"

It took a few seconds to sink in. And then it hit home as she remembered with crystal clarity the set of keys to her apartment that had been hastily dropped into the pocket of the pants in question. "Oh, George!" she cried. "You didn't!"

George shook his head ruefully. "It happens," he admitted.

"To an efficiency expert?"

"I was in a hurry. I guess I forgot to empty the pockets."

Andie couldn't hide her dismay. "You *forgot?*" she exclaimed. "The great George Demarest, who types messages on red three by five index cards, and files junk mail in alphabetical order? The same great George Demarest with the amazing measuring thumb? *You forgot?*"

"Don't worry," he said briskly. "I'm sure they're still in my pocket. We'll pick them up tomorrow as soon as the place opens."

"Tomorrow?" Andie was aghast. "And where do you propose I sleep until then?"

George gave her a dazzling smile. "That brings us to the good news," he informed her. "I assure you, Andie, your charms have not been showered upon me in vain." He paused, waiting for the power of his probing eyes to captivate her. "Tonight," he continued, as if bestowing a great favor, "you'll be sleeping with me."

"Sorry, lady, but there's no way I can break open this lock. You're gonna have to wait until you can get those keys from the cleaners."

Andie stood on the top landing at the entrance to her apartment and sighed miserably. In her hand was a yellow 3 x 5 index card with the words *Unbeatable Locksmith Company* typed neatly across the top. It was followed by a phone number and the slogan NO LOCK THAT CAN'T BE OPENED, which for some reason George had deemed necessary to include on the card. She repeated it to the locksmith, but he just shrugged.

"Oh, I can open it all right, but it ain't just the lock," he explained. "It's the way it was put on. It's bolted from the inside. I gotta drill all around it, and then if you're real lucky I might be able to replace it with a new lock." He shook his head and patted the door with his hand. "But this gorgeous door will get totaled."

George came up the steps with Speedy in his arms, lugging a collapsible stroller behind him. "How's it going?"

Andie looked at him murderously while the locksmith reviewed the problem once more for George's benefit.

"A most efficient lock," was George's only comment.

"You're wearing out that word," Andie cut in, but George ignored her. Taking the yellow card from her hand, he readjusted Speedy in his arms and jotted the name of the lock on his index card.

"Shouldn't you type it?" Andie asked sarcastically.

George ignored her again. "How much for the visit?"

"Twenty-five," the man said, and George wrote that down, too, before taking out his wallet to pay.

"I can pay my own bills," Andie said.

"This one is mine," he retorted. "Just like that terrific dress you're wearing. You know"—he grinned—"if that's all you have to wear, I'm enjoying every moment that I see you in it."

The locksmith started to laugh, but Andie's chilly glance stopped him. "Well," he said lamely, "if you don't need me anymore, I'll be off." He picked up his tools and began to head down the stairs.

"So," George said jovially, "it looks like you and I are in for a very interesting evening together."

The locksmith heard this remark and doubled back, handing Andie a card. "Just in case you change your mind," he said, casting a baleful glance at George. He disappeared down the stairs once more, leaving them to ponder their next move.

Chapter Four

THERE WAS A SMALL, weighted silence, broken finally by Speedy.

"More choc-vit?" he asked hopefully.

George laughed and looked at Andie. "Shall we make the best of it? I have exactly the same size kitchen you do. Would you like to try it out?"

"I thought I was invited to dinner," she answered, still ruffled. "Now I have to cook it?"

"Are you actually willing to chance *my* cooking?"

She recalled the TV dinners and sighed. "You do have a point. All right," she announced, "tonight we'll have southern fried chicken. Which means we have to go shopping before the stores close. That refrigerator of yours is . . . inefficient."

He lifted an eyebrow. "It was operating at peak efficiency this afternoon."

"That's the trouble with you," Andie said as they got

51

ready to leave. "You use efficiency as an excuse for ineptness."

"Ineptness? Are you for real?" He lifted Speedy onto his shoulders and headed down the stairs. Andie grabbed the stroller and followed, letting it bump down the steps behind her. "What do you say to that, fella?" George said to Speedy. "Am I inept?"

Neither of them seriously expected Speedy to answer, but the little boy scrunched up his face and seemed to ponder a moment. "Yes," he answered finally, after obvious deliberation.

Andie and George looked at each other and burst out laughing. "Well, he sure told me," George said, throwing her a conspiratorial glance. Andie felt her annoyance fading fast. The rapport between them had blossomed with that one small joke.

A minute later, they were walking up Columbus Avenue, surrounded by the eclectic small shops and the whirlwind of people. Andie realized that they looked for all the world like a typical young couple out for a walk, pushing their toddler in a stroller. She also had to admit that she liked the feeling very much. It was like playing house, but with grown-up stakes attached. However, her enjoyment was qualified by the sobering knowledge that Speedy's mother was still missing.

Stealing a glance at George's handsome profile, she wondered guiltily where Mindy was and why George had done nothing to find his cousin. He looked perfectly composed, as always, as if any problem could be solved with mere timing and good judgment. He could be utterly charming when he wanted to be, and she was sure that he knew it.

He obligingly played host, pointing out all the places of interest in the neighborhood, and for the first time since arriving in New York, Andie started to really examine her surroundings. It had been easy to overlook the frenetic variety before; she had had too much else on her mind. Moving in and meeting her new boss had taken all of her attention. But now, as she ambled slowly along with George as her guide, she saw that she had moved to a veritable bazaar of goods and cultures.

Every block was crammed with alluring merchandise. Even a simple drugstore had its charms, with nineteenth-century wooden shelves and apothecary bottles still lining the stucco walls. Within three blocks, they had passed stores that sold nothing but Hungarian pastry, windup toys, imported umbrellas, designer shoes, Japanese flower arrangements, Italian wine and cheese, and take-out Cajun food. The avenue was dotted with restaurants of every size and description—from the large and lavish to a humble pizza parlor.

And the variety wasn't just in the stores. Andie could hardly believe the people. They walked with the rhythm of the city, electricity alive in their gait. She saw every conceivable kind of attire, from faded jeans and punk paraphernalia to sleek European suits and designer brief-cases.

By the end of their shopping trip, she was loaded down not just with groceries, but with the new and stimulating anticipation of this unpredictable city.

"It's like a three-ring circus!" she exclaimed as they arrived back at their brownstone. "I've never seen so many people in one place in my life. Heck, it's like walking through an obstacle course."

George smiled knowingly. "Too much for you all at once?"

She put her shopping bag down on the stoop and looked around. "Hell, no! I love it!" The sun was on the horizon, casting a comfortable orange glow across the street. Somewhere nearby someone was playing a violin, its rich timbre underscoring the transition from the work day into the evening. Up and down the street, people were still coming home from work. A tiny old lady was walking two huge Dobermans along the curb, and right next door two little boys were playing marbles on the stoop.

Andie smiled, pleased at what she saw. New York would sometimes be maddening, she realized, but it would never be dull. She looked at George radiantly.

"I take it you approve of our neighborhood?" he asked.

"Oh, I approve, all right. It's nothing I could ever have imagined." She eyed him impishly, adding, "But then, neither are you."

"Is that good or bad?" he asked as he adjusted Speedy on his shoulders.

"Well, let's just say that you're probably the strangest person on this block."

"Hah!" he protested, genuinely surprised. "Now, that's where you're wrong. Wait until you meet some of the rest of the characters who live in our building. Next to them, I'm the Good Witch of the North."

This was not necessarily good news. Something warned her not to tease him too much more. After all, he had come to her rescue. And now that the crisis was over, there was no reason to back away from him. This very attractive man was attracted to her, she was sure of it. All she had to do was play her cards right, and the evening could very well turn out to be successful in ways she would never have thought possible, especially after only one day in New York. Things certainly did happen fast here, she thought.

"Okay, George," she said cordially, giving him a hint

of a wink, "I'm all ears. Tell me about the characters in this building. Then I'll decide if you hold first place for being the strangest." She picked up the shopping bag and was about to resume her travels to his apartment, but he stopped her.

"See that door below these steps?" He pointed rather ominously down under the stoop to a metal gate. Beyond it there was a door leading to the basement apartment.

"That's old man Barnes' place," George explained.

"So?"

"So, no one has seen him in six years."

Andie looked at George for a second to make sure he was on the level. Then she bent over for a closer look at Barnes's apartment door before looking back at George. "Six years?" she repeated. "Are you sure the guy is alive?"

"The only proof that he's down there is the mail he takes in and the enormous pile of newspapers and magazines that he throws away at the end of each month. The guy must read every magazine ever printed. It's an incredible pile. You'll see. Just wait till the end of June."

"Well, that's strange," she allowed archly, "but you're still a contender."

"Wait, there's more."

Andie started to climb the stairs when suddenly someone behind her began yelling at the top of his lungs. It was so startling that she was compelled to turn and look. There in the middle of the street was a young man bellowing up at someone in one of the brownstones across the street.

"DARYL!" his voice boomed loudly. "DARYLLLLLLLL!!!!"

Andie looked beseechingly at George.

"Another contender," George offered as he pointed

up to the top floor of the building across the street.

"DARYLLLLL!!"

The window opened and a young man looked down and threw something out of it. It landed with a clink on the sidewalk, and the man in the street scooped it up and disappeared into the building.

"That's Daryl up there," George said. "His intercom doesn't work, and he can't buzz in his guests, so—"

"So they yell up for him and he throws down the keys and they let themselves in. Sounds reasonable enough."

George laughed. "You think so? Wait a few more weeks before you make a final judgment. Just wait."

"When did his intercom break down?"

"Oh, about four years ago." Andie gave him a startled look, which he ignored. "New York is a fast-track town except when it comes to getting your landlord to fix something."

Andie didn't get it. "Why doesn't he just fix it himself? Back home, if something broke, my daddy would take care of it straight away. No sense depending on other folks to do it for you."

"Uh—yes," he agreed and then laughed weakly. "But don't hold your breath waiting for Daryl to fix it."

Finally inside, George pointed out the first apartment. "The Hernandezes' place," he said as he began the long climb up the first flight of stairs. "Do you like salsa?"

Andie was baffled. "I never ate it," she called up to him.

"You don't eat salsa," he laughed. "You listen to it . . . whether you want to or not." He trudged up the stairs, still explaining. "The Hernandezes recently bought a new stereo. Unfortunately, they only seemed to have enough money left over for one record, which they like to play—

a lot." He stopped and looked down at her for emphasis. "A hell of a lot."

Andie made no comment, but when they reached the second floor, she detected a sweet, heady aroma. Incense, that's what it was.

"Ummmm," she breathed. "Now, that smells great." She looked at the nameplate on the door. "Sheila Neuman."

"Ah, yes, Sheila," George said. "Our resident guru. Every so often she throws a weekend party for the local chapter of the Swami Brhavtahambu. It consists of five hours of chanting with accompanying sitar, cymbals, and drums. Makes the Hernandezes seem like a welcome relief." He pointed to the door opposite Sheila's across the carpeted stairway. "Candida's place." George grimaced. "She's an aspiring actress who has never actually acted in anything. Every so often she practices singing her scales. That's when you realize why she's never landed a job."

Andie absorbed this information wordlessly. "Anyone else?" she asked cautiously.

George gestured up the stairs to the apartment opposite his own.

"So who lives there?" Andie asked curiously.

"Thea Beaumont," he said. "She's a literary agent. Works in her apartment. I don't usually see her; she told me she's usually on the phone, yelling at someone about money."

They both laughed, and having finished his introductions, George marched up the stairs to his floor with Andie right behind. She caught up with him just as he opened his door. "Ahhh," he said, looking around his utterly perfect apartment, "normalcy, at last."

*   *   *

An hour later, Andie was relishing a scene of perfect domestic bliss. Speedy had eaten a scrambled egg and some blueberry yogurt and had been given a bath and put into his pajamas, and she was in the kitchen, cooking up a batch of fried chicken, corn, and biscuits for herself and George. Peering into the living room, she saw George reading Speedy a story as the child sucked placidly on his thumb.

". . . and the Mama Bear said, 'Who's been sleeping in *my* bed?'"

"I go bed?" Speedy chirped.

"Hold your horses, kid," George said as he turned the page. The two were stretched out on the sofa bed, George's arm casually draped around the little boy, and Andie was struck by how tender George looked doing this simple task. She strongly suspected that there were many deeper sides to him than the ones he had allowed her to see so far.

"And when Goldilocks woke up and saw the bears, she ran from the bed and out the door." He closed the book, adding, "The end."

"End," Speedy echoed sleepily. He took the book from George and studied it with a sober expression. For the first time, there was actual silence in the apartment.

The welcome lull made Andie look forward to the evening with a little thrill of anticipation. Something was going to happen between them, she just knew it. George might be unpredictable and he might be quirky, but he certainly wasn't shy. The pleasant feeling of playing house had intensified now that they were inside. And outside, the vibrant, eclectic city was still churning, its evening noises punctuating but not intruding on her activities. George's apartment had three long, narrow bay windows and Andie could see part of the darkening northern sky. "It still feels strange to be in a big city. The noises never seem to stop," she remarked half to herself, but George heard her and responded empathetically.

"They never will," he assured her as Speedy climbed contentedly onto his lap. "That's why they call New York the city that never sleeps." His hand unconsciously stroked Speedy's hair into place, and the little boy responded by snuggling closer.

"But does anyone ever sleep?" she asked uncertainly as a door slammed somewhere down below.

"You'll get used to it." He grinned. "Trust me."

Andie stopped her work and watched them for a moment, the dynamic man and the tired little boy. She wished she could take a picture of them at that moment. She also suspected that George had no idea how rapidly Speedy had earned a permanent place in his heart. Taking care of a toddler was constant work, but then there were moments like this. . . .

A dark thought marred her reverie. "George . . ." she said. "Have you—I mean, does anyone know that Speedy is here? Besides his mother, that is?"

He frowned. "No. Why should they? Whom did you have in mind?"

Andie slid a tray of biscuits into the oven and turned the burners down on the fried chicken and ears of corn. Facing the archway into the living room, she said what was on her mind. "I'm talking about the authorities, George. Have you faced the fact that Speedy is an abandoned child?"

"I don't know that he's actually abandoned," he said defensively. "Mindy could show up at any time."

"But still . . ."

"Look, I'm a blood relative. Why shouldn't he stay

with me for a while?" His arms tightened instinctively around Speedy, and Andie's heart contracted.

"Oh, I think he should," she said softly. "He definitely should stay with you—for a while. It's just that—well, maybe someone ought to be informed." She took a deep breath. "Like the police."

George looked away with a fierce expression. "Forget it," he bit out. "Things are fine just the way they are. This isn't the first time Mindy has pulled a stunt like this."

"It's not?"

"No," he answered rather smugly.

Andie was surprised, but she had sensed that there was more to this story than George had let on. She sat down, gesturing for him to continue.

"Mindy's never really been a mother to this kid," he said. "She got pregnant when she was sixteen, and her mother—my aunt Dorothy—took in Speedy and cared for him. Mindy went off to a special boarding school, which she barely scraped through, and treated Speedy like a baby brother who had dropped down the chimney. Things would have been all right, but Aunt Dorothy died six months ago." He sighed and Andie listened sympathetically. "Let's just say that Speedy has had a lot of bad breaks for a kid not even out of diapers."

He looked down and realized that the child had fallen asleep. "Shh," George put a finger to his lips. Andie tiptoed over and carefully lifted Speedy up so that George could pull out the couch and make a comfortable bed for him. When he finished, she laid the child gently down, and George covered him with the blanket. They looked at each other for a long moment and then turned out the light and retreated into the kitchen.

"Here," she whispered, handing him a pair of tongs,

"turn over the pieces of chicken. I'll check the biscuits, and when the corn is ready, I'll make a salad."

"Very efficient."

Andie playfully covered his mouth with her hand. "I'm warning you, George. If I hear you say that word one more time..."

He laughed. "But I mean it. I've been watching you cook. I'll bet the taste matches the preparation."

"Sir," Andie fluttered, broadening her accent, "you're about to enjoy a fust-rate, good ol' home-cooked southern meal."

George surveyed her handiwork and pouted. "What, no grits?"

"Grits are for breakfast," Andie said seriously.

He was standing right next to her, his alert presence dominating the small kitchen. Suddenly, she found it absolutely necessary to busy herself with the cooking, checking the corn one more time before covering the fried chicken.

George watched her with quiet appreciation and the hint of a smile. "Everything under control?"

She shot him a startled glance. Somehow it seemed that she should be asking him that question, and she said so. "You know, George, for a man who just had a tremendous responsibility dumped in his lap, you certainly are taking it all in stride." She studied him for a moment more and then bluntly asked, "Why?"

His eyes glinted for a moment, but his face remained inscrutable. "It's just something I wanted to do."

Andie squinted at him shrewdly. She knew his nonchalant facade was covering a human being with real depth and feeling. Her face softened as her gaze pierced him knowingly. "Why?" she asked again, her tone conveying a wealth of understanding. Don't get glib with me, George, she was saying. Tell me what's going on inside.

George studied her and she could tell he was struck by her sincerity. She knew there was no backing away from that luminous gaze of hers when she really wanted the truth from someone. George was no exception.

"Let's just say that Speedy and I have a common background, with one major difference," he said. "He knows who his mother and father are."

Andie's eyes widened in surprise, but George put up his hand and waved her reaction away. "There's nothing to get melodramatic about," he insisted. "I'm an adult."

Andie was still highly sympathetic. "It couldn't have been easy for you." She hesitated. "Do you . . . know where you were born?"

George shrugged. "I was told it was Appalachia or some such economically depressed area. My mother was not much older than Mindy. She gave me away when I was a month old."

Andie melted. "Then what happened?"

"Look, Andie," he said, putting his hands up. "I'm not going to bore you to death with some phony sob story. It's been a great life. I have no regrets."

"I don't believe you. There must be some bitterness, some anger—"

"At what?"

"An unhappy childhood! You can't convince me—"

"What unhappy childhood? I was put up for adoption, and was adopted in five weeks by Mr. and Mrs. Jonathon Demarest. They were a happy middle-class couple living in a typical middle-class suburb. I went to a typical high school, where I played basketball and worked on the school paper. I then went on to a typical American college, where I had a typical long relationship with a very nice girl who broke it off to marry someone else. After a typical short time of finding out what I wanted to do, I settled on a typical big city and went about pursuing the typical American dream. I had one more typical relationship, which ended typically. And lo and behold, here I am, standing in my kitchen, watching you look at me with that hungry gaze."

Andie gulped and looked away. Okay, so she couldn't foist any heavy emotional problems on him. But his attachment to Speedy was undoubtedly connected to his own experience. And nothing would ever convince her that he was typical. He was the most extraordinary man she had ever met—and the most riveting.

"What about you?" he asked curiously. She looked up and saw that he was watching her, his eyes a smoky gold.

"Me?" Andie gave him a slow, secretive smile. She had nothing to be secretive about, really, but at that moment she wanted him to think that perhaps she did. "I'm just your typical southern belle, complete with church socials, long, lazy summers, and great down-on-the-farm cooking. My pets were a horse named Pretzel, a prize cow named Annabelle, and an old hound named Thatcher my daddy gave me on my sixteenth birthday. Until this morning, the biggest city I'd been to was Washington, D.C., on a class trip in high school. I went to Duke University, where I majored in creative writing. After graduating, I landed a job writing for *The Uncle Wiggly Kiddy Hour* in Winston-Salem. Uncle Wiggly was a good ol' southern boy when he wasn't on camera, and I got involved with him in more ways than one. Then he got another job on a soap opera, playing the part of a shell-shocked veteran who gets the heroine pregnant. He invited me to write for that show, and I did—until last Friday."

George looked quizzical. "What happened to Uncle Wiggly?"

She shrugged. "The show died a natural death. I had ambitions, wanted to get out of my nice safe little environment and move to the big city. David—that was his real name, not Uncle Wiggly—knew he couldn't stop me. By the time I left, he was involved with someone else."

George lifted an eyebrow, impressed. "So now you've hit the big time, right?"

Andie shrugged again, pretending not to notice that his eyes had sent a provocative message. "This new show has very low ratings and could be canceled. They need fresh ideas, and I guess you can't get fresher than me." She smiled at him and a silence settled between them, but it was a comfortable silence, heavy with promise. "Dinner's ready," she said softly a moment later.

"Good," he answered, but neither one of them moved. George came toward her, closing the inches between them, and suddenly he was kissing her, his hands pressing against her shoulder blades. He took his time despite the rising excitement, which only made it all the more exciting. They were alone and they had all the time in the world. George's mouth sought hers with knowing determination, coaxing her and molding her into response.

But Andie didn't need coaxing. The combination of tenderness and strength that emanated from him was powerfully arousing. She wound her arms around his neck, drawing him closer, her heart beating wildly against his chest. They clung together, the kiss sending them into a vortex of private warmth.

Her eyes fluttered open, looking at him with shy curiosity. Had he been as shaken with that one kiss as she had? The vulnerability she read on his face told her that he had, and she thrilled with the knowledge. Desire was claiming her, shooting darts and arrows into her blood. His head lowered and he took her mouth again, his hands molding her waist and then dropping to hold the swell of her hips.

When the second kiss broke, they looked at each other for a long, timeless moment. Andie struggled to get a grip on herself. They had the whole evening in front of them. She didn't want things to progress too quickly, and she knew that prolonging was much more seductive than instant gratification. She gave George a mysterious feminine smile and took a step back. "The biscuits are ready," she said huskily. George said nothing but watched as she bent to retrieve them from the oven. They were a little browner than she had intended, but he didn't seem to notice. His eyes were busy traveling over all of her slim, petite figure, devouring it.

The table was set less than ten feet from where Speedy was sleeping, and they took care to tiptoe past him as they carried the food inside. George surveyed her handiwork appreciatively.

"Looks great," he said, and she wasn't sure if he was referring to the meal.

"Shall we?" she asked.

Andie's chair scraped the floor as George pulled it out, making Speedy blink and turn over.

"Shh!" she whispered, pointing at the sleeping child.

"This has been the most unreal day of my life," she whispered back. George's gaze was hot enough to melt a stone, and his thumb rubbed provocatively across her palm.

Andie stood up for a moment to turn out the one remaining lamp and to light the two candles she had placed on the table. Instantly, they were surrounded by an intimate glow, and George immediately claimed her hand again as she sat down.

The sounds of the city continued, but they seemed welcome and even friendly now. A bus lumbered by down below and a dog barked somewhere, and Andie felt that she belonged. A blessedly soft breeze floated in through the window, calming them and lulling their spirits.

"I can't believe I'm really here," she whispered.

"Shall I prove it to you?"

"How?"

"I want to kiss you again."

She giggled, deliberately slowing down the momentum that was galloping between them. Everything was happening so fast. She didn't want to rush into anything—not anything as promising as this. "Not yet, George. I mean, not now. Let's eat first, and—"

"Don't be nervous, Andie. I'm going to have you, one way or the other. If not tonight, I'm a very patient man."

Andie could think of nothing to say, and her heart thudded deliciously as he bent forward and took her head between his hands. "You're like a little southern sprite who's been sent to torment me," he informed her, lifting tendrils of her reddish hair between his fingers. "I'm not even sure if you're real, but I definitely intend to find out."

Andie was completely spellbound. Her lips parted unconsciously and her eyes half closed as he placed his mouth over hers. The reverie was cut rudely short by a resounding shriek from the street.

"DARYL!!"

"Oh, no," they groaned in unison, their eyes flying open.

Over on the couch, Speedy blinked a few times and threw a small fist over his face.

"HEY, DARYLLLL!" The shouting actually shook the windows. "DARYLLLLLL! HEY, DARYLLLLL!!!"

It was too late. Little Speedy shot upright in bed, took one look at the dining-room table laden with food, and made an instant decision.

"I hungwy!" he announced. "I eat!"

Chapter Five

"OKAY, SPEEDY, SIT DOWN." George plunked three phone books down on a chair between Andie and himself and plopped Speedy on top of them. His tone was amiable, but with an underlying tension. Andie perceived that he was as disappointed at the interruption as she was, but that he still wanted to make the best of it. Fair enough, she thought. They could still have a civil meal. And later, when Speedy was in bed...

A plate of corn and chicken, cut into bite-sized pieces, had been placed on the table, and Speedy dug in as if he hadn't eaten a thing all day.

"I don't know where he puts it," George remarked.

"He's a growing child."

George sat down and whipped his napkin onto his lap once again.

Speedy immediately lost interest in the food and concentrated instead on one of the candles. "Oooooh, pretty lights," he said cheerfully, reaching out to touch the flame.

"Careful," Andie warned. "Hot!"

George stopped him abruptly and lifted up the two candles, placing them out of reach.

"Now, where were we?" he asked as he reached across to take her hand. "Oh, yes, I was saying something about—"

"Watch out! The wineglass!"

It was too late. Speedy had managed to tip it over as he reached for the basket of biscuits. The wine ran across the table and began heading for the edge before Andie quickly caught it with her napkin.

"No harm done," she said brightly. And pointing at Speedy, she added a warning. "Young man, if you want anything else, please ask."

"Milk?" Speedy said promptly.

George jumped up. "I'll get it. You just keep an eye on him." On his way into the kitchen, Andie handed him the wine-soaked napkin.

"You know, George, maybe we ought to wait until Speedy is finished before we resume eating," she suggested.

"Nonsense," he said as he returned with a paper cup filled with milk. He placed it in front of Speedy and reseated himself. "There, now, that's not so bad." He tasted a piece of chicken and nodded enthusiastically. "Mmmm, it's delicious."

"Thank you."

They continued eating for another tenuous minute before Andie decided to try a stab at real conversation. She was still edgy about Speedy's presence, but she couldn't stand another minute of this silence.

"So how long have you been in business?" she ventured.

"Not that long," George said. He bent down to retrieve some chicken that Speedy had dropped on the floor. "I had been working as a manual systems analyst for a large company for over ten years. Then they fired our entire department without any notice."

Andie's eyes darted back and forth as she half listened to George while simultaneously keeping an alert vigil on Speedy's actions.

"To make a long story short, I had trouble convincing anyone to match my previous salary."

"So you decided to go out on your own," Andie concluded rather hurriedly as she pointed at the sharp knife Speedy was reaching for. George grabbed it away, which brought a howl of protest from Speedy.

"I need it!" he cried. "I need it!"

"No, Speedy," George said firmly, placing the knife on the other end of the table. "This is dangerous. Yes," he said to Andie, returning to the topic she had started. "I figured it was time to go it alone. Besides, I had been toying with the idea for a while. Getting fired was like a good swift kick." He looked down and neatly caught the plate that Speedy was just about to push off the table.

"Jord, I want more," Speedy said.

"More what?"

"This." Speedy pointed at George's plate.

"I don't think he's hungry at all, George. He's just overtired."

"This! I want this!"

George looked murderously close to losing patience altogether, but he swallowed his annoyance gallantly. "Okay, Speedy, if you insist." He tried cutting Speedy some more chicken, but instead of eating it, the child threw it across the table. Two pieces landed in Andie's wineglass, splashing the front of her new dress.

"Oh!" she cried, dabbing at her dress. "Terrific, just what I needed." She blotted the wine and gave George a dire look. "I'm telling you, that kid is tired, not hungry."

George looked at Speedy. "Are you going to eat this chicken?"

Speedy shook his head vehemently and pushed the chicken around on his plate. Then he picked up a piece and stuffed it into his mouth.

"There," George said haggardly. "Now, that's not so bad."

Andie gave him a suspicious look.

"Anyway," George resumed the conversation, "the irony was that the very company that fired me ended up being my first client."

"He who laughs last, huh?"

"Budda?" Speedy chirped. "I need budda." *Budda,* Andie translated absently, was Speedy's pronunciation of *butter.*

"Actually, it makes perfect sense," George continued, doggedly ignoring Speedy's request.

"Budda?"

"I had ten years experience with them. So obviously when they needed an outside consultant, I won the contract hands down. I charged them my previous full-year salary," he said proudly, and gestured at her to drive his point home. "Now, that's irony."

"Ooooh," Speedy exclaimed. "Very pretty." Suddenly, without warning, he climbed right up onto the table and crawled, putting his knee right into the butter.

"Catch him," Andie said tersely. "Quick."

"Gotcha," George exclaimed, lifting him back onto the phone books.

"I need it, I need it!" Speedy hollered, fidgeting with

unearthly shrieks as George tried to clean him off.

"This is ridiculous," Andie snapped over the squall-ing. "He's not hungry."

George shook his head. "You heard him. He needs it, he needs it."

"What? He needs *what?*"

"Good question!" George said and, putting his arm around Speedy, asked again. "What do you want?"

"This!" Speedy pointed at the candles.

"The candles?"

"Cambles," came the affirmative response.

"No," Andie said automatically.

"No," George repeated. "Too dangerous."

Speedy let out a bloodcurdling scream and then con-tinued with a long series of sobs, alternating with de-mands. "I need it! I need it!"

"This is all Daryl's fault," Andie said. "I'm going to hog-tie that idiot and all his stupid friends for waking up this child."

"I need cambles," Speedy sobbed.

George loosened his grip, which was a big mistake. In the next instant, Speedy made a mad dash across the table, upsetting nearly everything on it. Chicken, plates, corn, wine—the place was a mess.

"That does it," Andie said, losing her temper. She looked at the toddler in George's arms and issued a direct order. "Young man, you get back in your seat immedi-ately."

She turned irritably to George. "He needs a regular high chair or a seat. You can't keep putting him on a bunch of telephone books and expect him to stay put."

"Why are you blaming me?" George raised his voice. By now he had lost his cool as well. He gave her a stern look. "It was your idea to cook this big fancy meal. I

would have just used TV dinners, and that would have
been easy to take care of. But noooo, you have to go
and get creative on me."

"A high chair is efficient, Mr. Expert. Telephone books
are not."

Speedy grabbed a piece of chicken and threw it on
the floor, giggling wildly at his success.

Andie picked up the remaining piece on the platter
and tossed it onto George's plate. "Here, eat this before
it gets cold."

"It is cold. It's been cold for fifteen minutes now."

"Cold," Speedy echoed. "More chicken!"

Andie took a deep breath. "This is hopeless. You can't
have a normal meal with a two-year-old around."

Again Speedy saw his chance. He made a beeline up
and across the table, but Andie was too quick for him.
"Gotcha, you little devil!" She looked at George and
uttered a final command. "To bed."

George scowled. "Now I understand why they call
this age the terrible two's."

"I seep now, Jord?" Speedy asked plaintively.

"He's tired," George translated tersely. "He wants to
go to sleep."

"No kidding."

"Seep?" Speedy repeated earnestly. "Go seep?"

"Yes," Andie agreed. "Go to sleep now. As a matter
of fact, we'll all go to sleep." She stopped in midsen-
tence, Speedy in her arms, realizing the delicacy of what
she had just said. She looked around the apartment fur-
tively, but George was oblivious of her concern.

He was busy clearing the disastrous dinner from the
table in a most efficient manner. Finally, he noticed her
unease. "What are you looking for?"

"A good place for you to sleep." Her eyes challenged him, but he didn't respond. Instead, he threw her an amused glance. "You wouldn't happen to own a fold-out bed or cot or sleeping bag, would you?" she persisted.

He didn't answer, which only made her more nervous.

So he was going to be difficult about this. She should have known. "Maybe a bunch of thick blankets piled one on top of another?" she tried.

"Sorry, but I only have one bed," he said, pointing in the direction of his bedroom. "I don't generally entertain overnight guests—who sleep in the next room, that is."

Andie flushed and peered into his bedroom. The bed was a standard double one, large enough for two but definitely small enough to encourage togetherness. She swallowed hard. Maybe the urbane women George was accustomed to meeting were more aggressive than she was, used to fast relationships with immediate intimacy. But she wasn't like that, and she wasn't about to change now.

"There are a bunch of my shirts hanging in the closet," he called from the kitchen. "You can use one to sleep in tonight."

Big of you, she thought, contemplating her alternatives. She noted the locksmith's telephone number on the index card lying on his desk. Either she spent a small fortune breaking down and then repairing her door, or she slept with George. Either way she was in for a very interesting evening. A hotel was out of the question. After the money she had had to lay out for two months' rent in security, not to mention the whopping fee to the rental agency and the movers, one night in a hotel would break her. She simply couldn't afford it.

She looked at Speedy cradled comfortably in her arms. His eyes were practically closed and she realized how exhausted she was herself.

George bustled in and extracted Speedy from her arms.

"Come on, kid," he whispered. "We've all had a very tiring day."

"Yes," Andie agreed fervently. She watched as George placed the child onto the couch and readjusted the pillows around him. Speedy nestled snugly under his blanket, warmed and soothed by George's gentle ministrations. George *was* good with him, Andie realized. And good *for* him, too. She watched as he kissed Speedy softly, then tiptoed back to where she stood at the foot of his bed.

"Well, that's that," he whispered. "I'm beat." He grinned at her mercilessly and began unbuttoning his shirt. "Bedtime." She returned his grin with a stony stare that accomplished nothing. George ignored her plight and sauntered into the bedroom, loosening his tie and draping it casually over one arm. A second later, he reappeared with one of his fresh shirts, which he threw across the room to her. She caught it and watched wordlessly as he took off his own shirt, affording her a delicious view of taut, lean masculinity. Then he strolled back into the bedroom, leaving the door open.

He was doing this on purpose, she knew. They had both looked forward to a romantic evening, and it had been ruined. He had no right to take it out on her! Unless he was using that as a convenient excuse to get her into his bed. She sighed heavily and retreated into the bathroom, locking the door.

She was able to stall for several minutes as she hid in the bathroom, getting ready for bed. But eventually she had to emerge, clad in George's crisp starched shirt, which hung only to the middle of her thighs. Speedy was out like a light, and George's bedroom was dark.

She stepped cautiously inside, wondering what she would find, and felt a stab of dismay when she made out George's long, virile figure tucked neatly beneath the covers like a mummy in a case. She couldn't tell if he was wearing anything, and she didn't want to find out.

"George?" she whispered, but he didn't stir. "George, are you awake?" she asked with growing concern. Still no movement. She hesitated and then strode boldly into the room and stood next to what was supposed to be her side of the bed.

"I don't like this arrangement at all," she whispered, just in case he was really listening.

She sat down carefully on the edge of the ultrafirm mattress and debated with herself. Suddenly, an idea came to her and she almost laughed aloud.

Of course, she thought gleefully. How very simple. *And* efficient! She restrained a chuckle, then proceeded to swing around and lie down on the bed—head to feet. She managed to pull the covers out from where they had been neatly tucked in at the foot of the bed, and snuggled beneath them.

"Good night, George," she said happily and patted his feet. "Pleasant dreams."

Again George did not stir. And he would no doubt have remained placidly immobile throughout the night if it hadn't been for the rude awakening they got twenty minutes later.

Just as Andie finally found herself drifting off, the most ear-splitting music suddenly burst into her consciousness. It reminded her of a Latin dance club she had been to once in New Orleans. Trumpets were blaring in rich harmony, accented with a persistent bongo beat.

Then a chorus of Spanish singers joined in, harmonizing lustily.

At first she thought it was part of a dream, but then she realized it was all too real.

"Whazzat?" she murmured sleepily.

A crash of bongos jolted her to an upright position, and she found herself looking at George face-to-face. She was totally perplexed, but George seemed to be admiring the ingenious system she had devised for sleeping in the same bed with him. His amused eyes swept over her rigid form, stopping at her sleep-startled face.

Andie stared back at him, wondering how on earth Speedy had managed to sleep through this racket. Suddenly, comprehension flooded her face. "The Hernandezes!" she cried.

George nodded. "And they're playing our song, dear. 'Los Caballos de Madrid.'"

Andie was awestruck. "It's so loud. Doesn't anyone ever complain?"

"Everyone," George said. "Just wait."

Sure enough, a voice, loud and angry, cut through the noise to dominate the street.

"Hey! Hernandez! Turn that music down! Now!!!"

A few seconds went by and the voice repeated the command. "Hey, Hernandez! I'm warning you!" Mercifully, the music was turned down, leaving the usual sounds of the city to dominate the night.

Andie fell back in relief. "Thank God," she sighed to the unseen voice.

George punched his pillow into perfect submission and prepared to go back to sleep. Andie was still staring respectfully out the window. "Thank you, kind soul, whoever you are," she said.

George turned his head and gave her an odd-looking smirk. "That kind soul," he said calmly, "was Daryl."

Andie's first week in New York was a kaleidoscope of new impressions. Her job was scary at first, then challenging, and finally stimulating, as she met dozens of new people and settled into something that resembled a routine.

George and Speedy remained a part of that routine. Somehow that first night had set a precedent, and she found herself having dinner with the two of them more often than not.

Every evening she would rush home by six, trudge up the flights of stairs, and find a neatly typed note from George on her door. "I bought a huge roasting chicken. Hope you know how to cook it." "Can you take him on Saturday at two?" "How long does it take to boil an egg?"

After the one hapless night together, she found that George, surprisingly, stayed at arm's length. She didn't know whether to be relieved or disappointed, but except for a few quick kisses on the landing, the physical intimacy between them was on hold. They became instant best friends, generally too harried or simply too exhausted to consider anything else. Of course, the attraction was still there, lying in wait, but it had to stand in line. The priorities allowed no room—and no time— for placing their personal desires above the constant demands and needs of the omnipresent two-year-old who so effortlessly dominated their lives.

Andie found it was a great relief not to have to cook in her own apartment that first week. She still hadn't unpacked, hoping to get to it over the weekend. Her bed was set up and the majority of her furniture was in place, but most of her belongings were still hidden away. After opening a dozen boxes, she managed to find all of her clothes, but that was it.

In all this time, Speedy managed to be the center of everything. And meanwhile, Mindy never phoned.

"You're going to have to face reality, George," Andie said on Friday. "You are not equipped to handle a two-year-old. It takes a permanent commitment, not to mention a realistic schedule and the patience of a saint."

They had just put Speedy to bed, and George stood over the sleeping child with haggard eyes.

"Well, you don't have to sound so sanctimonious," he said. "You'll have *your* chance starting tomorrow. Don't forget you promised to take care of him over the weekend."

Andie nodded. Speedy would be hers for two days while George went to Syracuse on business. She examined him sympathetically. "You look exhausted, George."

"Appearances are deceiving," he said as he took her by the arm and led her around to his bedroom. He plopped on his bed and stretched out, looking up at her with a woebegone expression. "I passed exhaustion on Tuesday. What you see before you is utter despair."

"But you're not ready to throw in the towel, right?"

He managed a competitive grin.

"And you said *I* was stubborn as a mule." Andie sighed. "I'll bet you haven't gotten a drop of business done all week."

"I haven't," he admitted. "Although I did try. Take Monday, for instance. I got three important calls, and Speedy howled through each of them." He sighed heavily. "Can you imagine what it's like to be on the phone with a crying baby in your arms? There I was, trying to convince my client to spend a huge sum on revamping a division, and I had to excuse myself in order to extract Speedy from the dumbwaiter, which he had somehow climbed into, don't ask me how." He threw his arms across his face and groaned.

Andie plunked down next to him. "What else happened today?" she asked. They had become adept at exchanging daily stories, both appreciating the outlet and the sympathetic ear.

"You tell me," he said. "Did you finally figure out what to do with Foster's new wife now that his old one has returned from the dead? What's her name—oh, yes, Fredonia. Boy, that's a good one."

"You've been watching our show," Andie said in surprise.

"What else do I have to do while folding Speedy's clothes and making him lunch? I'm just your typical homemaker. Incidentally," he pointed out, "one of your sponsors is a client of mine."

"Really? Which one?"

"Dusty Dan, the all-purpose waxer. There was a production problem at the Jersey plant, and I had to go in and work out the kinks. Now they're making wax at peak efficiency. Great stuff," he said and pointed at his newly waxed floor.

Andie tried to imagine George working out a knotty problem at a factory with Speedy dangling over his arm and winced. "Face it, George," she said worriedly. "You need help."

"You mean a baby-sitter?"

"I'm talking about professional advice," she said

slowly, taking his hand. "I'm sure the city has specialized agencies equipped to handle this sort of thing."

He jerked his hand away and looked at her as though she were a traitor. "I'm all the help Speedy needs," he said. "If Mindy doesn't want her child, then I'll take care of him."

"How?" Andie tried to reason with him. "Look at yourself. You're exhausted, overworked, and frustrated. You can't do it alone. You need help, and Speedy needs a real family, not an efficiency expert."

"You don't know what you're talking about," he growled, but he averted his eyes, unwilling to face her.

"I do, too, and you know it," she insisted. "I'm not saying you shouldn't take care of him. All I'm saying is you can't keep going on like this. It's not good for you, and it's not good for Speedy, either."

George was clearly annoyed. "What's that supposed to mean? Are you saying I'm not fit to be a parent?"

"On the contrary," she said, taking his hand again. "You are the best thing that ever happened to Speedy. I admire you for it."

"Then what the hell is your problem?" he demanded.

She threw her arms up in frustration. "You're avoiding the inevitable, George. Speedy has to be accounted for, sooner or later. You can't keep hiding out with him, without going through the proper legal channels."

"You make me sound like a criminal," he said. "What's the rush? When and if Mindy shows up, I'll deal with it then. In the meantime, why create problems? A lot of red tape is the last thing I need right now."

"That's just the point," she pressed. "What if Mindy suddenly shows up next year and wants her child back? What are you going to say? That you found Speedy on a doorstep and got amnesia for a year? Isn't it going to look awfully strange that you never reported it?" She sighed heavily. "The longer this goes on, the deeper the complications get."

"Don't you worry about complications," he said, turning to eye her coolly. "I'm an expert at complications, you know."

"Oh, I've noticed," she said with a little smile, backing down a little. She didn't mean to attack him. She only wanted to help. "And I meant what I said about you and Speedy," she added quietly. "Honestly, George, you're wonderful with him. I—I've never seen a man so tender and caring with a small child."

There was a pleasantly weighted silence after that remark, during which Andie could almost reach out and touch the electricity that rose between them.

"Thank you," he said softly. He reached out and touched her hand, stroking it gently. "You know, it's been only one week, but I feel as if I've known you a lifetime."

"Listen to how quiet it is now," Andie noted after a more lengthy pause.

"Yes. Daryl's friends are all safely locked up somewhere, the Hernandezes work late, Candida has a voice lesson on the East Side, Sheila is off in the mountains with her guru, and Speedy is fast asleep."

They both looked over at the sleeping child, who was resting placidly with his thumb in his mouth. A slight breeze came through the open window, bringing the promise of tranquillity, but a tension rose out of the peacefulness, bringing an even greater promise for them. George leaned toward her and she met him willingly, her arms twining around his neck. The kiss was slow and mellow, as natural and right as the breath of summer in the air.

"I've been waiting for a long time," George murmured

against her cheek.

"I know," she whispered back. "But Speedy . . ."

"It wasn't just him," he said, leaving a trail of gentle kisses along her throat. "I wanted to be sure you were ready."

She said nothing, lowering her eyes as his gaze fastened on the skimpy halter top she was wearing. Suddenly, it seemed like no covering at all, and she was keenly aware of her breasts trembling beneath it.

George kissed her again, his hands molding the soft skin of her back as she clung to him. The strong but gentle hands moved up to her neck, deftly unfastening the knot that held her halter top in place. The brief garment fell forward into his lap, baring her small, pert breasts to his hungry eyes.

Andie's eyes dropped demurely. She had always worried that her breasts were too small, her figure too boyish to be considered really sexy. But George seemed to read her mind, contradicting her fears with a masculine awareness that thrilled her. "You're exquisite," he whispered, tracing a delicate line around each creamy breast and winding a sensual circle around each rosy peak. "So soft and yet so firm. You don't need a bra at all."

It was one of the advantages of being small-breasted, but she had never thought of her breasts as exquisite. And yet one look at George's rapt face convinced her that they were. Fascinated and proud, she moaned with delight as he leaned forward to taste one pink nipple, sucking it gently and teasing it with his tongue.

The slow, rhythmic motions ignited her. She gripped his shoulders helplessly as he continued to arouse her, moving leisurely to the other breast and bringing it to the same peak of awareness. Feeling fully and deliciously under his command, she fell back on the bed, letting him cover her once again.

His hard, smooth arms went around her, and she felt the crush of her breasts against his chest. It felt so wonderful to be with him like this, exciting and sensual and yet somehow safe, all at the same time. She trusted him, she realized, as he dropped kisses over her cheeks, her nose, her chin. She trusted him and she wanted to open her heart to him. The awareness caused her eyes to open with wonder.

"Jord!" a little voice called from the other room.

"Oh, no," George groaned, his head jerking up.

"Jord! I woke up!"

Andie smiled resignedly. "No rest for the weary," she quipped. She sat up and tied her halter top back in place. "It's all right," she whispered, catching the sight of George's disappointed face. "This wasn't the best time or place, anyway."

He nodded reluctantly. "I know that." Then the glint returned to his eyes, and he clasped her hand before getting up to answer Speedy's call. "When I make love to you, Andie, we'll be completely alone. And," he added huskily, his eyes smoldering with certainty, "we'll take all the time in the world."

Chapter Six

MONDAY MORNING ON THE SET of *Until Tomorrow Comes* was the scene of a real-life crisis. The new star actress had just been injured in a weekend boating accident, and the entire day's script had to be rewritten.

From what Andie learned in the gossip mill, the actress had suffered a concussion, and the new script was needed by eleven that morning. To make matters worse, George was supposed to have flown back to New York on Sunday night in time to relieve Andie of two days of baby-sitting. But the last she had heard from him, his plane had been grounded because of fog on the runway, and he had promised to take a train instead. By Monday morning, he still hadn't shown up, and rather than call in sick, Andie decided to chance taking Speedy to work with her.

Heading through the busy morning hallway, she managed to spirit Speedy into her office and close the door before anyone saw her. The next thing she did was to dial George's number and leave a message.

"Greetings," George's answering machine clicked on. "You have reached the office of Demarest Consultants. No one is in at the moment, but if you'd like to leave a message—"

"Boy, would I ever," Andie muttered anxiously.

"Wait for the sound of the tone. You'll have time for a sixty-second message. The tone will be along in exactly three seconds."

She waited impatiently until the piercing sound of the beep came through the line, and wasted no time in delivering her message. "This is Andie, you creep. You promised to get back by eight this morning. That's very inefficient of you. It's also downright irresponsible. Do you realize I've been with Speedy since Saturday afternoon? It's my second week on the job and we've got a crisis here at the studio." She paused for a second as she thought of an appropriate ending. "HELLLLLLP!"

She slammed down the receiver and looked at Speedy, who was playing with her Magic Markers. He had just drawn a crooked mustache on his upper lip and was busy adding sideburns when she interfered.

"Please, George, call," she prayed aloud as she wrestled the marker out of Speedy's hand.

Her intercom buzzed, making her jump.

"Hey, Maguire!" Her boss's voice was like a jolt of electricity so early in the morning. "Did you hear the bad news?"

Speedy was reaching for the marker again and she let him have it rather than have him cry while she was talking to her boss. "I heard," she responded tensely as Speedy happily made a mess of himself.

"Writers' meeting, five minutes, conference room. We've got less than two hours to rewrite today's script. That leaves a half hour for rehearsal and then we go on—live."

"Live?"

"Yeah, live. What's the matter? You're not getting cold feet, are you?"

"Well, we should be able to come up with something in that time."

"I want it ASAP," he responded and then clicked off without saying good-bye.

Andie gulped and looked at Speedy. "Please, George, come quick."

There was a sudden knock on the door, and Gail Conway came in. She was a tall, willowy young woman, with exactly the kind of figure that Andie had always wanted. Andie had liked her at once upon learning that Gail had always wanted a petite, boyish figure like hers. Gail had a small but durable part in the soap that had kept her steadily employed for years. She already knew all about George, and seemed only mildly surprised to find a child sitting on Andie's desk.

"Don't ask," Andie said, scrubbing at Speedy's face.

"I'm asking." Gail charged in and plunked down, took Speedy onto her lap, and finished the job of cleaning him off while Andie regained her composure. Speedy seemed to accept Gail as an ally, for which Andie was grateful. "I take it this little one belongs to the infamous George," Gail said.

All Andie could do was nod miserably.

"It seems that George is taking slight advantage of you, wouldn't you say?"

Andie threw up her arms and sighed. "What can I do? I'm a jerk, I admit it. But he really needs help."

"What he needs," Gail injected, diverting Speedy with an eraser from the desk, "is a real baby-sitter."

Andie's mind darted back to Friday night, when she and George had been intimately entwined at his place. If Speedy had been with a baby-sitter and they had been free to go up to her apartment... "I guess he's afraid to leave Speedy alone with a stranger," she said, avoiding Gail's eyes.

"Well, I'm no stranger," Gail said cheerfully. "Could you two use a free Saturday night?"

Andie's face lit up with gratitude. "You'd do that, Gail?"

"Sure, for a small favor."

"Name it."

"In exchange, you have to rewrite the script so that I don't have to marry that creep of an actor Lou just hired. He's such an oaf. Every time he kisses me on the set, he goes much farther than he has to, if you know what I mean." Andie grimaced sympathetically, and Gail shuddered. "Ugh! I can't stand the idea of playing opposite him in bedroom scenes for a whole season."

"I don't know," Andie said hesitantly, causing Gail to stab herself with an imaginary knife. "I'd not only have to convince the other writers, but Lou already said he wants you two in some steamy scenes..." She thought it over. The prospect of a night alone with George was very tempting. She could fix him her specialty, shrimp gumbo, and homemade pecan pie for dessert. She looked up at Gail and smiled. "I'll see what I can do. Maybe I can have you catch the creep two-timing you."

"Thank you, thank you, thank you, from the depths of my heart. But right now you have a bigger problem." Gail grabbed Speedy's fist, which was about to smear Magic Marker over that week's script. "I'll take Speedy off your hands right now, and he and I can get acquainted." She bounced him on her knee a little to reassure him. "By the way," she continued. "Just out of curiosity, what are you going to do about our missing character? Fredonia's just shown up. You can't write her out yet. She was supposed to be a big deal."

"Well," Andie mused, "as far as the new script goes, we can always conveniently get her into a car accident. Then all we do is wrap up another actress in face bandages, put her in a hospital bed, and keep her in a coma until the real star is ready to go back to work."

"Which leaves you short of a main plot."

Andie scrunched her face as she toyed with a few ideas. "All we need is a new element to push the plot forward. Maybe a little mystery."

Gail tried to help out. "How about introducing another woman to come along as a mistress, so that Foster can feel nice and guilty, not only about his new young wife but also about the old one in bandages?"

"Nope," Andie said, nixing it quickly. She was watching Speedy as he once more started drawing on her script. "That's too much, and it's not believable, even for a soap. What we need is a mystery." She racked her brain. "Now, why did Fredonia disappear?"

"She cracked up?" Gail tossed out.

Andie shook her head. "Overdone."

"She thought she was dying?"

"Too corny."

"Amnesia?"

"Give me a break."

Their thinking was cut short by Speedy, who somehow managed to tip over all of Andie's pens and pencils. They spilled onto the floor, causing him to cry in frustration, and the script fell along with them. Andie looked at him and sighed. "You wouldn't have any ideas, would you, Speedy?"

"Crayons!" he said, pointing down at the mess.

Suddenly, Andie's whole face changed. She was looking at Speedy as the wheels in her head began to pick up speed. "Oh, Speedy, you are wonderful!" she exclaimed.

"You look like you're on to something," Gail said.

"Maybe." She looked at Speedy in a trance as the idea began to take form in her brain. "No, not maybe, but—" Her face lit up. "Yes, it's possible."

"Possible sounds good."

"Try definitely."

"My favorite word," Gail said.

Andie beamed at Speedy, as if he had really come up with the idea himself. "It should work," she said to herself, calculating quickly.

"Well, what is it?" Gail asked, excited. "What did you come up with?"

"Shhh." She waved Gail off and quickly began to jot down her ideas on paper. "Brilliant," she whispered aloud as her excitement rose. "It's absolutely brilliant—and so simple." A moment later, she raised her head, beaming with creative energy. "Speedy, you're a champ."

Gail was about to open her mouth when Lou Collier came storming through the door without knocking. He was obviously very nervous and distraught, and he didn't even notice Speedy, who was now sitting on the floor.

"Hey, Maguire," he barked. "I thought I told you we had an emergency meeting. What do you need, an engraved invitation? Let's move it."

"I think I came up with something already, Lou," Andie explained excitedly, used to her boss's antics by now.

Collier lifted a brow. "Okay, let's hear it—and it better be good. I've got no time for mistakes. This disaster could put us in an early-ratings grave." He turned to lean against the wall and saw Speedy for the first time.

"Hi, man." Speedy smiled, throwing a pen at him.

Collier dodged it and pointed sternly at him. "Hey, what's this kid doing here?"

"He's our newest addition to the plot," Andie said, covering quickly. She went on with her idea without missing a beat. "Fredonia's been gone for two years, right?" Collier nodded curtly and stared at Speedy as Andie continued. "Well, unknown to anyone else, she had a baby two years ago, and has been raising it secretly. But now she's in the hospital in bandages and might die." Andie looked at Collier's granite face. He was still looking at Speedy. "The big question is—what do we do with the child?"

"Yeah, what do we do?" he asked suspiciously.

"The answer is, the father has to take it. But the sixty-four-thousand-dollar question is—who's the father?"

Gail nodded supportively. "Sounds good to me. But I'm just a player. What do you think, Lou?"

Collier scratched his chin and didn't answer for a moment. Then he nodded slowly. "Yeah," he agreed thoughtfully, finally tearing his eyes away from Speedy. "Not bad at all." His eyes squinted and he nodded more forcefully. "We can do a whole thing where if the real father doesn't come forward, the kid has to be put up for adoption. It'll be a real tear-jerker." He straightened up and clapped his hands together, obviously relieved. "Good work, Maguire. That takes some of the pressure off. The next thing you have to do is call the city office for abandoned children, and get all the info you can. I want to make this as authentic as possible. Then get your butt down to the meeting." He favored her with a grin. "You're okay, Maguire." She basked in the praise but almost jumped at his next question. "But I have one more thing to ask you. How'd you get the kid here so fast?"

Andie gulped. "Uh—do I have to answer that?"

Collier thought quickly. "No," he said. "Just make sure you show up in my office in fifteen minutes with the information I need. Oh, and have the kid's parents sign the release forms." He turned to leave and stopped. "And from now on," he said sternly, "don't go hiring any actors. I don't care who they are, that's not your job."

Andie nodded weakly and waited for Collier to leave before falling back in her chair in a cold sweat. "Phew," she breathed, wiping her brow.

"Nice going," Gail said. "You just killed three birds with one plot. The script is saved, Speedy has a reason for being here, and you and George get a night off, compliments of yours truly. Not bad for a morning's work." With that, Gail picked up Speedy and headed for the door. "I'll take the kid, you get on the phone, and then you'll be free for your meeting."

Andie took a deep breath and reached for the phone book. But she barely had a chance to open it when there was a knock on the door. "Come in!" she called, without looking up.

"Hi," said a familiar voice. She looked up, startled. There stood George, obviously winded. Her face gladdened at the sight of him, despite her annoyance that he was so late. She had somehow forgotten how appealing he could look, and how reassuring his mere presence could be.

"I finally made it," he said, looking around her office. "Uh, where's Speedy?"

Her eyes took in his exhausted features. "He's with my friend Gail down the hall."

"Terrific, I'll just head over and get him, and be on my way."

"Oh, no, you won't," she said quickly. "You won't believe what's going on here." Andie stood up and walked briskly around her desk to face him. "Now, listen, and don't talk until I'm finished. You've got to cooperate and I've got very little time in which to explain everything."

But George couldn't stop. "Look, I'm sorry I'm late, but I couldn't get a train, and—"

"George, please! Just sit down!" She pushed him into the chair in front of her desk and stood over him.

George looked at her guiltily. "You must think me terribly irresponsible."

"Up until a few minutes ago," she said ominously.

"But now something has happened to change all that, right?" he asked hopefully.

"Something like that."

"Good, now you sit down." Before she could stop him, he reached up and pulled her onto his lap.

"George, I can't now," she protested, but her tone was weak and she knew it. It felt so good to be this close to him again. She reasoned that she could explain everything to him just as well sitting comfortably on his lap.

"What's the matter?" George asked. "What's the big rush?"

She lifted the script from her desk and waved it in front of his face. "This," she said. "I've got only two hours left to rewrite it, so let me go."

But George only nodded and held her tighter. "Maybe they need a good efficiency consultant around here." He took the script from her hands and began flipping through it, while Andie remained willingly imprisoned in his grasp. "What's the problem?" he asked mildly.

"I'm not kidding, George. We have some very important things to discuss, but I can't talk now. Among them are Speedy, and my job, which may hang in the balance."

But George paid her no heed. Instead, he began leafing through the script until he came to an interesting part. "Will you get a load of this!" he exclaimed.

She tried to get up, but he held her down as he pointed to a line in the week's now-canceled script. His eyes lit up as he read the words to himself. "Wow! This is pretty risqué for a daytime soap. Did you really write this?"

"Yes," she said slyly. "Why?"

He looked at the script and then up at her. "This is hot stuff, Andie." His eyes twinkled. "This script was made for me."

"Well, I've got no time to audition you."

"And why not?" He pulled her close, glanced down at the script, and then into her eyes. "'Oh, darling, darling,'" he read histrionically. "'Don't you see that you and I were brought together by fate? No matter what else happens, we belong together.'"

"Stop it!" Andie cried. She glanced at her watch and pleaded with him. "Please, George. Don't you understand, I'm late."

"But I can't help myself." He continued reading. "'In the past few days that I've been away, I've thought of nothing but you. I've missed you so much.'" His face was inches from hers, his eyes mesmerizing her with their intensity. "'You know how you drive me mad when we're alone.'"

"You're crazy, you know that?" she protested.

"Am I? I doubt it. After all, these are your words."

He glanced once more at the script and his eyes lit up. "Aha, the good part is coming. Would you like to see your part?"

"I know the part," Andie sighed. "I wrote this scene, remember?"

"Then you know what I'm going to do next." He put the script on his lap and took her face in his hands. Andie lost her resolve at that moment as she gazed into his tawny eyes. She hadn't seen him for days, and until he had walked in the door, she hadn't admitted to herself how much she had missed him. She had thought she'd want to strangle him, but now that he was this close to her, she practically melted under his touch.

He glanced down playfully at his next line. "'I know how much you want me,'" he said forcefully. "'You know it's true. Admit it.'"

"This is not funny, George," Andie wailed. "I'm in the midst of a major crisis and you are not helping. What if someone should walk in right now and see us?"

"Then this is what they'd see."

He drew her into his arms and kissed her, letting the heavy script fall to the floor. Andie's head fell back in surrender as his tongue found its way into her mouth, and she clung to him hungrily. The kiss lasted for a deliciously long time, as if there were no research to do, no phone call to make, no meeting to attend.

"You know something?" George asked as he dropped a series of tantalizing kisses along the side of her neck. "This is the first time you and I have been alone together. No Speedy." His voice dropped to a husky whisper. "I like it."

"Me, too," she answered, her green eyes level with his. George smiled and brought her hands up to his mouth, kissing each one. The simple gesture brought up a well of response in her. If only they could slip away right now and be alone for a long, long time . . .

"I mean it, Andie," he said seductively, turning her hands over to kiss the sensitive palms. "Don't you feel the tension gone? It's just the two of us now, alone."

"I'm glad you like it," she said, "because I have a surprise for you." His eyes sparkled above her two hands, still imprisoned in his. "Dinner at my place, Saturday night," she announced. "Minus one child."

"What?"

"You heard me. This is strictly an adult affair. Gail will baby-sit, and you will show up at my door promptly at eight. Until then, I'm afraid I won't have much time for you or Speedy. I'll be so busy that I don't want to make any dates I'll have to break."

"Is that my punishment for being late?"

"No," she stated point-blank. "It's my salvation. I've got a sixty-hour work week facing me, and I won't want to do anything at the end of the day but go to bed. I mean to sleep," she added hastily.

"I see," he said after a moment. His eyes darkened. "Then how about one more for the road?"

"It will have to be a good one to last a whole week," she answered breathlessly, her face already angled toward his.

Their mouths met in an uprush of longing. George crushed Andie against his hard, lean body, as if to memorize every alluring curve and valley. Then his hands slid down the sides of her body, molding it possessively, and at last they settled provocatively on her hips. They were just beginning another rapturous kiss when the door banged open.

"Hey, Maguire!" Lou Collier shouted, unannounced. "Where the hell is that kid's mother? I need this contract signed, and—" He stopped and stared at them. "What's this, more research?"

Andie jumped off George's lap and hastily adjusted her dress. "Lou!" she exclaimed. "You could at least knock."

Collier looked at George without acknowledging Andie's remark. "Who are you?"

George didn't miss a beat. "Why, I'm the kid's mother, of course."

There was a long moment of silence, during which Andie stifled a grin and a sigh of relief at the same time. Then Lou jerked a thumb at George. "Well, follow me into my office. I need you to sign this release form. We'll just use your kid for today's show." He turned to Andie. "Did you get that information I asked for?"

"Right away," she answered crisply. "I just got a little . . . sidetracked."

"Yeah, well, get moving. The other writers are already going over your idea." He crooked a finger at George. "Come on, sidetrack," he said. "In my office."

She watched them leave, George turning to wink before the door closed. Although it was going to be a long week, her spirits lifted as she thought about the weekend. She could sleep late on Saturday, and then she and George would be blessedly alone. That thought gave her the energy to face the day's work.

A few minutes later, she was reaching for the phone book when a voice startled her once more. "Hey, Maguire!" She jumped at the voice on her intercom. At first it sounded exactly like Lou, but it wasn't.

"Nice work, getting us a baby-sitter for Saturday night. I'm looking forward to our little rendezvous."

"George!" she scolded. "You'd better behave yourself. I mean it. At the rate we're going, I'm going to face unemployment before too long. Where's Lou, anyway?"

"He left me here and headed to that writers' meeting to get something. Meanwhile, I thought we could continue our most interesting discussion."

"I told you, George, I've got work to do." She clicked off the intercom and began thumbing through the phone book when temptation got the better of her. Once more her finger pressed the talk button. "Oh, darling," she cooed. "Are you there?"

But it wasn't George's voice that answered. "Knock it off, Maguire. You've got a rewrite to get to me by eleven. And make sure you call that city office! You got that—darling?"

"Oh, uh—yes, Lou." She removed her finger from the button as if it had been electrified. "What a day," she moaned, shaking her head. She thought about it for a moment and added, "George is in for it now."

As she picked up the phone book and looked up the appropriate child welfare agency, the alarming sequence of events ran methodically through her mind, like specific flash cards that would eventually reach a logical conclusion.

She came to New York. She met George and Speedy. Instantly, she became involved in both their lives. George went away. She took Speedy for the weekend. George was late getting back. There was the mishap with today's script and she came up with using Speedy in it as a last desperate measure. She located the number she was seeking and dialed it, a nameless discontent making her feel suddenly cross.

A voice answered mechanically, and all at once everything fell into place. Her hand shook for a moment and the receiver rattled back into the cradle. Whom was she kidding? Maybe this call was supposed to be for research purposes only, but deep down she knew that she and George couldn't continue this farce with Speedy any longer. They couldn't keep juggling everything so precariously. Today she had managed to wriggle out of her predicament, but what about next time, and the time after that?

More importantly, what about Speedy? Was all of this really fair to him? She had no idea what the authorities would do, but what if they took Speedy away from George? As painful as that would be, wouldn't it be better to know now what the future would hold? What if Speedy formed a deep attachment to George and *then* had to be taken away from him? The thought of his sweetly disheveled face made her heart contract.

Something had to be done. Speedy's mother had to make some kind of concrete decision about her child, once and for all. Either she had to shape up and take care of him, or she would have to allow him to go to a strong, loving home where he could have a real family and a chance for happinenss. Something else occurred to Andie as she considered Mindy's disappearance. Maybe Mindy hadn't contacted George because something had happened to her. She could be injured, or ill, or—God only knew what.

Resolutely, Andie picked up the phone and dialed the number once more. "Uh, yes, hello. Is this the New York Department of Children's Social Services?" she asked. "My name is Andie Maguire," she began cautiously. "I'm inquiring about the legal process of what to do when a child is—"

She stopped. Did she really have the right? She remembered George's fierce determination to keep Speedy at all costs. But would doing this really prevent him from doing just that? It was entirely possible that they would gladly let him keep Speedy, that he would have no trouble at all proving his sincerity and his worth.

She took a deep breath and continued. "Uh, yes, I'm still here." She swallowed hard, and after one last brief moment of doubt, she committed herself to the task she had taken upon herself. Her voice took on a new firmness that was only edged with the slightest touch of sadness.

Gathering her courage together, she spoke clearly into the phone. "I'd like to report an abandoned child."

Chapter Seven

AFTTER PUTTING IN A SEVENTY-HOUR work week, Andie collapsed on her bed Friday evening and didn't wake up until almost noon the next day. Not even the combined efforts of the Hernandezes, Daryl's friends, nor Candida's singing could wake her from a much-needed and deserved sleep.

She finally rose to what she referred to as the weekend buzz, the sound of the city at play. Radios blared, children shouted, and cars double-parked as they loaded up for trips to the beach or the country. But for her it was a day to relax and plan the all-important dinner for herself and George, to which she had been looking forward all week.

She had conveniently managed to push the call to Social Services aside, pretending for the time being that she hadn't interfered. The woman she had talked to had been calm and sympathetic, and had made it clear that several days would probably go by before anything would happen. There was a great deal of red tape involved, and the situation Andie had described was not potentially life-threatening. Having done what she considered the right thing, Andie decided to let the matter take care of itself.

Savoring the glorious weather, she pushed her hanging spider plant aside and leaned out her window, peering down at George's window just below.

"Good morning!" she called down. "Yoo-hoo, anyone down there?" She looked across the street, where Daryl was just leaving his building. He had on a back pack and looked as though he were heading away for the weekend. Thank God, Andie noted to herself.

Just then George stuck his head out and looked up at her.

"Good morning," she greeted him.

"Good afternoon," he emphasized. "I've hardly seen you all week. Are we still on for tonight?"

"You bet your boots. Be prepared for the best shrimp gumbo north of the Mason-Dixon Line."

"I'll bring the wine."

"Just make sure that's all you bring," she said dryly as she pointed at Speedy. The child had managed to climb around George, trying to join him by perching on the ledge.

"Whoa, Speedy, be careful," George said in alarm. He grabbed the boy in time and looked up to face Andie's scolding eyes. "I guess I'd better keep these windows closed."

"Or put bars on them, Mr. Efficiency," she added. "It's called baby-proofing."

"I'll work on it," he said. "But it hasn't been easy this week. Speedy gets into everything. Every time I turn around, he's up to some mischief. This morning I found him hiding in the dumbwaiter for the fourth time this week."

"Just make sure he stays in one piece until Mindy gets back," she warned. Trying to sound casual, she added, "Has she called yet?"

He shook his head. "We'll talk about that tonight at dinner."

"Yes," Andie agreed, hiding her sudden rush of guilt. She hadn't heard anything more from Social Services, and now that she knew she was going to face George directly, she didn't see how she was going to put off the task of telling him what she had done. Suddenly she wasn't at all sure how he was going to take it, and her anxiety rose sharply. "See you tonight!" she called, ducking back inside.

But her optimism returned as she thought about the delightful evening in store for them. Maybe George would understand. He might even be glad that she had taken a definite step. There was no point in worrying about something that might work out after all.

After a hearty breakfast, she dressed in a plaid shirt and overalls and skipped down the three flights of stairs until she found herself standing on the front stoop. There she was greeted by a startling sight. Sitting in five huge neat piles were scores of magazines and newspapers. She stared for a second before remembering what George had told her.

"Barnes," she said aloud as she examined the mountain of periodicals. None of them was more than a month old. "Amazing," she murmured as she gazed one more time at the closed iron gates and wondered about the man who lived inside. "Well, at least he's quiet," she added as she looked across the street to one of Daryl's friends, who was beginning the now-familiar call up for the keys.

"DARYLLL!" he yelled several times. "Hey, Daryl!" But no Daryl appeared.

"He took off a few minutes ago," Andie informed him. "You just missed him."

The man started as if a ghost had addressed him. Then he shrugged, looked her up and down, and hopped back up the street. So much for Yankee courtesy, she thought.

She turned in the opposite direction, toward the myriad shops on Columbus Avenue. She had been so busy that she hadn't had time to explore them. Today she intended to remedy that, and the first item on her list was a dress that would knock the socks off Mr. Perfectionist himself, George Demarest.

That pleasant task took over two and a half hours of trying on fourteen outfits in eight different stores, but it was worth it. She pondered, compared, and marveled at the combination of wild, daring, and unerring sense of style she found everywhere. Finally, she settled on a black sleeveless jumpsuit that was cinched in at the waist to show off her petite figure. With it she bought black high-heeled sandals and large, clunky pieces of silver jewelry. After some hesitation, she also bought a black-and-silver lacy scarf to tie around her head, Madonna-style.

Checking her watch, she saw that it was already after four. She hurried to buy the ingredients for tonight's feast and rushed home with all of her packages in tow. By seven o'clock, the gumbo was simmering, the rice was boiling, and Andie Maguire's famous pecan pie was cooling on the windowsill. Her anticipation mounted as she took a fast shower and lavishly sprayed herself with cologne. She caught sight of herself through the fog on the bathroom mirror and smiled. Her cheeks were flushed and her green eyes were sparkling with a secret excitement. You know what's going to happen tonight, she admitted slyly to herself.

She took a deep breath and shook her hair around her face. Yes, she thought. And I'm ready.

George was already twenty minutes late when a disgruntled Andie finally decided to go downstairs. It was either that or let her impatience mount until she exploded. She was sure George wouldn't stand her up. After all, he was easy enough to find. He only lived one flight of stairs away.

Probably Gail was late, she reasoned. He'd be up any minute. But after another five, she decided to investigate. When she knocked on his door, Gail was there to answer it.

"Well, hi," Andie said dubiously.

"Hi, yourself," Gail snapped.

Andie hesitated. "Uh, is there something the matter?"

"In a nutshell—yes." Gail leaned against the doorway and held up five different-colored index cards. "Do you know what these are?"

Andie nodded. "I've had some experience with them," she said as her friend began to shuffle them like playing cards. She held them out like a magician.

"Pick a card, any card."

Andie was reluctant to go along, but Gail was insistent. Reaching out, she drew a red card and examined it. "Emergency numbers." She shrugged. "What's wrong with that?"

"Nothing," Gail answered. "But he's managed to cover every conceivable kind of emergency, from swallowing poison, to cuts, broken bones, head injuries, and asphyxiation—with the name and phone number of each hospital that specializes in that particular problem."

"He's just being responsible, that's all. I think this emergency card is very thoughtful."

"The card may be, but not the lecture series that goes along with it. Your pal George should have been a college professor."

"Oh, no, Andie said. "I should have warned you. He's a little eccentric when it comes to Speedy's welfare."

"It gets better," Gail said, holding out the cards once more. "Go on, pick another one."

This time it was a blue card. One look made Andie burst out laughing. "These are diaper instructions," she said.

"That's right. And in case I can't figure it out, he *drew* instructions on the back for me to *follow*."

Andie examined the diagram on the back. "Good artwork," she commented. "Does this also come with a lecture?"

"And a demonstration as well." Gail held up the other cards. "Want to guess at the rest of these?"

Andie took them from her and glanced through them quickly. George had managed to cover everything from double-boiler bottle-warming to a list of Speedy's favorite bedtime stories, which he had cataloged in alphabetical order.

"Honestly, Andie," Gail complained. "Are you sure you know what you're doing? This guy's a good case for the nut farm. He doesn't trust *any*one. You'd think he was getting ready for a trip around the world, instead of a simple night out."

Suddenly, George called, "Oh, Gail, would you come here a second? I just want to show you how the phone works. I've preprogrammed the emergency numbers so all you have to do is push a button and it dials them by itself."

Gail looked at Andie and sighed. "See what I mean? He's crazy. The kid's real father couldn't be this protective."

"I'll handle this." Andie pushed her aside and marched into George's bedroom, where he was busy placing another index card by the phone. Speedy was in his arms, and after taking the child from him, she picked up the index card and examined it. All she could do was shake her head. "George Demarest, now you've really flipped. This is absolutely ridiculous."

"I was just—"

"You are overreacting to a simple, ordinary situation. You'll be right upstairs, not in Timbuktu. I've got a great dinner prepared that is going to grow old and die if we don't get up there and eat it. Gail is perfectly capable of dialing a phone, warming milk, diapering a two-year-old, and putting him to sleep. Now, are you coming, or do I have to drag you out of here?"

He looked at her sheepishly. "I guess I'm behaving like a nervous parent, huh?"

"It's normal reaction," Andie said, softening. "You just have a very bad habit of taking that normal reaction and adding your own kind of abnormality to it, that's all. I know you by now, but Gail doesn't." She waited to see if he would contradict her, but he merely stood there looking at her oddly, his head cocked to one side. "So what do you say? Shall we leave now?"

At those words, Speedy's face suddenly changed. "You go out, Jord?"

"Uh-oh." George's face also changed. "I think he's experiencing separation anxiety."

"No go, stay, stay," Speedy pleaded, beginning to whine. "Stayyy?"

"Come on, let's get going," Andie said, but George didn't budge.

"Maybe we ought to eat down here and—"

"NO!" Andie's loud voice made Speedy jump in alarm. "No," she repeated more quietly. "Are you crazy, George?

It's our first night alone together. Don't spoil it."

"Jord! You go out?"

George looked tenderly at Speedy, who stretched his little arms out. He lifted the little boy up in his arms, and Speedy grasped onto his neck for dear life.

"Here, give him to me," Andie said, wresting Speedy away. It took some deft plying, but finally Speedy was transferred, clinging now just as doggedly to her.

"Andie, you go out?" Speedy asked plaintively.

Andie took a firm hold on her emotions. "Why don't you leave first, George," she suggested. "I'll stay here and talk to Gail and then meet you upstairs."

"No!" Speedy cried. He panicked, kicking and squalling in her arms in an attempt to get back to George.

"Go, already," Andie ordered George. "He'll live. No child ever died from separation."

Bolstering himself against Speedy's screams, George marched over to the door. But he couldn't bring himself to leave. "Let me just kiss him good-bye, all right?"

Andie's heart contracted. Her face softened as she gave Speedy to him for one last kiss, but when she tried to take the child back, George, not Speedy, held on for dear life.

"Let go, George," Andie ordered.

"Look, are you sure we're doing the right thing? He really needs us. Can't you see that?"

"Let him go, George. He'll be fine once you leave."

"It's so hard to leave him," George admitted as he finally relinquished the child back into Andie's arms. "I guess I'm being a little overprotective."

"Terrific," Gail said dryly. "This is the first recorded case of adult separation anxiety. Will wonders never cease?" She shook her head at George and then gave him a push, sending him out the door. As soon as George was gone, Speedy buried his face in Andie's shoulder, crying as if his heart would break.

"Jord!" he screamed. "Jord! Jord!"

Andie felt a pang of terrible guilt but suppressed it as she reminded herself that his behavior was entirely normal. She comforted Speedy until he began to calm down. "Well, I guess I'd better get going myself," she said unconvincingly.

She tried handing Speedy over to Gail, but the same scene was reenacted with even more difficulty.

"Andie! No go, no go, no go!" Speedy sobbed.

"Well, what do you know?" Gail said in surprise. "The kid's really attached to you as well. I guess that bonding theory they talk about really works, doesn't it?"

Andie swallowed her emotion as she tried to put Speedy down. He immediately grabbed her leg and refused to let go. "You don't think that Speedy is starting to treat me like a—a—" She had trouble saying it, and Gail filled in for her cheerfully.

"Welcome to the world of parenthood, kid. We all get the instinct eventually. Only with you, the cart came before the horse."

"No go out!" Speedy wailed.

Andie knelt down and disengaged the winsome toddler from her leg as she took him in her arms. "Now, now, Speedy," she crooned. "I'm only going out for a little while. You let Aunt Gail take care of you, okay?"

"Nooo!" he sobbed, and tried to get hold of Andie's leg once more, but Gail was faster.

"Bye-bye," Gail said firmly, opening the door.

"Nooo!" Speedy cried piteously.

Andie hesitated. "Maybe George is right. Maybe I should—"

"Oh, no, not you, too!" Gail said. "Get out of here.

The sooner you leave, the sooner I can get him to bed. He's very tired. Can't you see that?"

"I know, but—"

"Go! That's an order." Gail marched her to the door and rudely shoved her out into the hall, slamming the door behind her. Andie was left standing alone in the hallway, listening to Speedy's cries, which were only partly diminished by the solid oak door. But when she turned shakily to head upstairs, there was George waiting on the landing, looking as guilty as she felt.

They looked at each other and he gave her a small smile and a wave. "Hi," he said.

They stood listening to Speedy crying and stared at each other wretchedly. The pitiful sound cut through Andie like a knife.

"He'll be fine," Andie said limply.

"Sure he will," George agreed.

"It's a normal reaction."

"Every child experiences it."

Neither spoke for a moment. There was an unbearable tension as they stood poised, both ready to rush back inside. Then a wave of relief swept over them as the crying slowed down and finally came to a halt.

Andie took a deep breath. "I guess he's all right," she said, trying to laugh.

His eyes captured hers, and she melted under the burning tenderness she saw there.

"Alone at last," George said.

"At last."

"You look great."

She went to him and they embraced lightly. "Hungry?" she asked.

He grinned, his eyes moving sensuously over her slim

form. "Very." Her chin lifted and their mouths came together in a brief, tantalizing kiss. Andie's blood was fired, but she withheld her desire for now.

"Let's go," she whispered. They both listened for a moment, but only silence ensued from his apartment. Holding hands, they dashed up the stairs like two kids playing hookey from school.

"Hey, this is beautiful," George said as he sat down and admired the table she had set. The candles had already burned down halfway, but the dinner was still warm, and nothing was the worse for wear. "I'd say this is going to be a first-class evening."

"With no interruptions," Andie added. "The Hernandezes won't be home until eleven, and I saw Daryl leave this morning for a weekend jaunt."

George added his own information. "Sheila is in the country with her guru, and Candida has laryngitis."

"What could possibly go wrong?"

"Nothing."

He took her hand and squeezed it. At that exact moment, Speedy let out a cry down below, making them both jump. They exchanged concerned looks and waited for more, but no sound came.

"Gail can handle Speedy," she assured him. "Shall we eat?"

They gave each other a slow, private smile. The whole evening lay ahead of them, ready to unfold its delights.

Andie brought out the first course, a chilled gazpacho that she had made in the blender. "A Spanish cold vegetable soup," she explained as she ladled it into two earthenware bowls. "Very refreshing in hot weather."

"Most efficient," George commented as he took a taste. "And delicious," he added.

Andie merely smiled, struck by the change in her reaction to George's remark. A few weeks ago, it would have irritated her. Now she found it almost endearing. It was so . . . George.

She beamed at him and began on her own soup, looking forward to the rest of the meal with confidence. Suddenly, her spoon was suspended in midair as the sound of a child crying reached them through the open window.

"What was that?" he asked tensely.

She didn't answer at first.

"Was that Speedy crying?"

"Maybe it was someone else's child," she hedged, not wanting to spoil the mood.

Again the crying began. George put down his spoon. "That's Speedy," he said, alarm creeping into his voice. "I'd know his cry anywhere."

Andie considered. "I'm sure Gail can handle him." She reached over and patted his hand. Then she went back to her soup, but George just sat there, listening.

"Look," she said, stifling a sigh, "if you're so worried, why don't you pick up the phone and call? Gail will tell you if anything is wrong."

He frowned. "I don't want to overreact. We only left a few minutes ago."

"True." She watched as he picked up his spoon and began to eat again, but she could tell his heart wasn't in it.

"I mean it, George," she insisted. "Call. Then your mind will be at rest and we can enjoy the evening without worrying."

"I don't want Gail to think I'm a lunatic," he protested under his breath, but he threw his napkin on the table and headed over to the phone, punching the numbers quickly. "Uh, hello, Gail, this is George," he began weakly. "No, no, everything is fine. Uh—is everything fine down there? Well, good. Oh, no, we just thought we heard Speedy crying, that's all." There was a pause, during which George looked decidedly uncomfortable. "Well, it doesn't hurt to check," he said defensively. "All right, see you later." He hung up, looking relieved. "She says he's fine. Wasn't crying at all." Sitting back down, he smiled at Andie as if he had known all along. "Now, where were we?"

Andie laughed. "I have to admit, George, I'm glad you made that call."

"Better to be sure," he said briskly.

"Right."

Suddenly, they looked at each other and burst out laughing. "We are really a couple of basket cases, you know that?" Andie said. "We're not even his parents." An uncomfortable silence passed, during which she realized that it was worse than that—they weren't even married.

"Maybe we should start thinking about full-time child care for Speedy," she suggested, filling in the gap. "After all, we both work and—" Andie stopped and groaned. "Listen to us!" she exclaimed, holding her head in her hands. "We sound like an old married couple."

"Let's face it, we might as well be," George said. "Ever since we met, we've been acting more like parents than friends. Or even lovers."

"But we're not," Andie made sure to point out.

He gave her an odd little smile. "Not what?"

"You know what I mean, George," she said, glaring at him.

"I know what you mean," he said mildly. "You are definitely falling for us."

"Us? *Us?*" She could hardly believe her ears. "What do you mean, *us?*" George looked blank. "There is a definite order to some things in this world, George. Don't you know that?"

But George was only half listening. His ears were pitched toward a more subtle sound than her voice. "Hold it a second," he said. "I thought I heard something down below."

Andie slapped her hand against her forehead. "You've got to get a hold of yourself, George. This is our first evening alone together. Please, don't ruin it."

He swallowed hard and shook his head. "I can't believe myself," he admitted finally. "You're right, I'm acting crazy. That kid has really gotten to me."

"He's hooked me, too," Andie confided. "It was just as hard for me to leave him. But he is not my child, and he's not yours either. And right now, he's in good hands. So let's eat, okay?"

"Fine." George tore off a piece of bread and buttered it, determined to continue the meal. "So, how are you going to resolve the soap next week?" he asked. "Does the real father finally show up?"

"Not telling," she teased. "We're on our honor not to divulge the exciting ending. You'll just have to keep watching for the next two months."

"I probably will," he said dryly. "By the way, that was some juicy love scene between Bart and Evelyn. You did write that, didn't you?"

"Maybe yes and maybe no," she said with a seductive wink.

George perked up. "I guess there's only one way to find out. We'll have to do some research later on." He attempted a casual tone. "Uh, what time did you tell Gail I'd be down later?"

"I didn't." Andie grinned. "Why?"

George didn't answer. He merely tore off another piece of bread and ate it.

"So how was your week?" she asked. She started suddenly as she thought she heard a baby cry. Stealing a glance at George, she saw that he hadn't heard anything. It must be her imagination.

"I played house," George answered readily, finishing his soup. "Speedy and I took a walk and we bought a toy boat. Then we went to the pond at the park."

Andie sighed miserably as she heard the cry again. What was the matter with her? This was ridiculous.

"Now what?"

"Oh, uh, nothing," she said, looking up at him from a daze. "Go on, you were saying something about the zoo."

"The park."

"That's right, the park."

He threw down his spoon. "You were listening for Speedy, weren't you?"

"No, I wasn't! I just thought I heard something, that's all."

George glowered. "Was this something coming from down below us?"

Andie squirmed. "Maybe later I'll give Gail a call to ease both our consciences."

"Why wait?" George practically leapt for the phone and dialed his number. They could both hear it ringing down below. Then a baby definitely started crying and George and Andie looked at each other.

"Now that *is* Speedy," he said, and straightened up as Gail answered. "Hi, Gail, it's me. Look, I'm sorry to bother you again, but—" His face dropped. "I'm sorry, I thought—" A second later he hung up the phone and looked at Andie. "She hung up on me."

Andie managed to laugh. "Well, we're driving her crazy. I can't blame her. Now, come on, George. Let's leave everything to her and really take advantage of this evening. No more talk of Speedy or Gail. I'll go and get the main course, and you open the wine."

She headed toward the kitchen, but stopped abruptly at a series of bangs that emanated from somewhere in the building. This was followed by a child's laughter, which was interrupted by an enormous thump. Andie and George both jumped in alarm. "What was that?" she cried.

"Probably Speedy falling off the couch," George announced ominously. "Let's go." He leaped up and headed for the door with Andie in pursuit.

"I knew this would happen," George shouted as he ran down the stairs three at a time. He already had his keys out by the time he reached his door.

"Hurry," Andie said as she caught up to him.

He got the door open and together they burst in upon a very surprised Gail. She was sitting on Speedy's bed, reading him a story. On the floor were three other books, clearly the source of the falling sound they had heard.

Speedy took one look at them and tried to rush toward them, but Gail stopped him.

"No go out!" he demanded.

"Out!" Gail ordered them as she wrestled with Speedy. "I mean it. If you two so much as say another word or show your faces here one more time, I'll quit." She ushered them back into the hall, snatching George's keys out of the lock. "For safekeeping," she explained craftily. "I'm locking you out for the night." Her face lit up in a coy smile. "I'm also taking the phone off the hook."

Speedy was still crying when Gail slammed the door in their faces.

"I guess we deserved that, huh?" Andie said sheepishly.

They listened, reassured, as Gail managed to calm Speedy down.

George leaned against the wall, a new resignation etched on his features. "If we're going to live through this night," he said somberly, "we will have to take our minds off Speedy by concentrating very hard on one thing."

"And what's that?" Andie whispered, although she already suspected the answer.

Reaching out and taking her hand, he pulled her into his arms. "This," he said, kissing her with sensual deliberation. The kiss deepened at once, surprising both of them by its intensity.

"You're right," Andie said, looping her arms teasingly around his neck. "We'll just have to concentrate like mad."

Chapter Eight

GEORGE LEANED BACK in his chair, the picture of satisfaction. "I've got to hand it to Gail," he said, stretching briefly. "That was the best meal I've ever had, and I only thought about Speedy once. Okay, twice."

Andie laughed. "I think we're cured," she said.

"You know what I could use right now?" he asked. She shook her head. "A nice cordial. Do you have any?"

"Coming right up." She stood up and headed toward the kitchen, but before she could get past him, he reached out and pulled her onto his lap.

"Wait a minute." She giggled. "I'll get some crème de menthe."

"That's not cordial enough," he said, shaking his head in mock disapproval. "I'm talking cordial as in bordering on intimate."

She smiled. "So much for the crème de menthe." They kissed, fired with an excitement that had been slowly building all evening—all week, Andie realized dimly as she settled into his arms. "Mmmm," she purred as the kiss ended. "Better than crème de menthe." Her eyes fell on the table. "Let me just get rid of this mess," she whispered, "and the remainder of the evening's agenda will be up to you."

He laughed seductively. "Fair enough. But I'll take care of cleanup. After all, you were the chef. Why don't you go ahead and I'll join you in a moment." He kissed her again, his tongue finding hers and teasing it into response. Andie squirmed deliciously on his lap and at last slid off, running off toward her bedroom before he could catch her.

The methodical clinks and bumps of an efficiency expert clearing the table were the only sounds in the small apartment as Andie slipped inside her bedroom and closed the door. She tiptoed to her closet and reached toward the back, seeking a garment she had once bought but had never worn. She had felt too self-conscious ever to wear it before, thinking she lacked the figure—as well as the nerve—to carry it off. But tonight she felt beautiful and wanton, unfettered by former inhibitions. She quickly slipped out of her clothes and got ready for George, who was just turning off the water in the kitchen.

Suddenly, everything was completely quiet. Then she heard his voice, a little uncertain in the stillness. "Andie?"

She answered him quietly, but her voice was charged with anticipation. "I'm in here, George." She sank back into the shadows of the room. "Turn out the kitchen light," she added.

A moment later, the whole apartment was sheathed in darkness, except for the candles burning low on the table. They lit a path directly to her room, and George followed it, opening the door to let in a feathery shaft of light.

Andie was stretched out on the bed when he appeared in the doorway, peering inside. His silhouette was compact and strong as he stood there, and a flood of desire washed over her.

"I can hardly see you," he whispered. "It's so dark."

"You'll get used to the dark. Come in, George."

He made his way slowly to the bed and sat down.

"There, that's better," Andie said, her hand touching his sleeve. "Would you like another cordial?"

His face changed, first with recognition and then with a seriousness tinged with sensual awareness.

"What's the matter, George?" Her voice was husky, pitched barely above a whisper.

"Nothing," he answered. "My eyes are adjusting to the dark. At first I thought I was merely imagining what I'm seeing now."

"Oh, but you're not." Andie's hand ran lightly up and down his arm, keenly aware of the unyielding muscle beneath the cloth. She let out a little sigh as he caught her hand and held it.

"You're like a mirage," he breathed in masculine delight. "That thing you're wearing—what is it?"

"It's a nightgown, George. Do you like it?"

His eyes swept over the confection of lace and silk that barely covered her. Then his hand began a sensuous journey that started at her shoulders, winding its way down across her breasts to her bare thighs. "I like it very much," he said hoarsely as his hand began gently lifting the hem. "But I'll like it even better when it's off."

His hands continued to graze her body as he lifted the scanty garment, pulling it gently over her head. She watched his eyes ignite as he looked at her body, thrilled with her power to excite him. "Beautiful," he whispered, drinking in her femininity. "You're like a wanton little sprite sent to earth to drive me mad."

Andie giggled breathlessly. "And you're the god of the forest . . . what's his name?" She closed her eyes against the rush of pleasure as his hands caressed her.

"George," he answered. "Obviously."

"Oh, of course." She laughed, arching her back slightly as his mouth descended to taste her breasts. "Oh!" The whimsical exchange was lost as she let herself swirl into the tide created by his sweet, knowing mouth. Its warmth sent a bolt of desire through her as her fingers tangled unconsciously in his thick brown hair.

George slipped out of his clothes quickly, letting Andie rake her hands down the smooth, hard planes of his chest. Her fingers danced over his body, tracing the slim hips, strong, narrow legs, and rounded, muscular arms. The butterfly movements aroused him tremendously, and he responded by returning each caress to her own softly rounded body.

"All fire and silk," he murmured huskily, parting her soft thighs with one hand. She cried out when he reached between her legs and stroked her sensitive core, already alive and ready for him. Now she was sinking deep into a cloud of pleasure. They were no longer on a bed in a room; they were floating somewhere above the earth. She reached through the blinding light of her own passion to touch him, delighting in the masculine shudders she evoked.

All at once his strong, hard body was covering hers, dominating her with its urgency. His mouth left a trail down her neck, across her breasts, and down to the sweetly rounded curves and valleys of her, bringing her to a pinnacle of desire that made her moan and shake with need.

Crying out with abandon, she flipped both of them over so that she was astride him. She sat up, positioning herself over his body, easing him inside her with one long, relishing stroke. Bent slightly forward so that her small, firm breasts hung deliciously before him, she began a slow, rhythmic dance. Her eyes closed mistily, but he stopped her, his eyes capturing her with sensual command. "No," he insisted. "Look at me."

She looked and saw clearly what she had dreamed of seeing—a completely passionate, giving man. A strong man, a lovable man—the man she loved. A current of awareness sprang up between them, like a live wire that tightened and intensified as they moved.

Andie drank in the waves of feeling until she could bear it no more. Then she fell forward, her hair flying across his face, her breasts crushing against his chest. George's strong arms tightened around her, holding her close, and together they spun wildly out of control.

They were silent for many moments afterward, George's arms still enclosing her protectively. Her mind continued to float effortlessly, but one thought stood out with lovely clarity. This moment was beautiful, she thought. Absolutely and utterly beautiful. She and George were a single unity; they fit together perfectly.

Deep, deep down she knew that this union was meant to be. It was only a matter of time before that recognition would surface. But in the meantime, there was still the question of Speedy hanging in the balance.

When Lou Collier burst into her office on Monday morning, Andie was deliciously lost in thought. She was trying to determine the exact moment at which she had fallen in love with George Demarest, but found that she couldn't quite pinpoint it. Had it been when he had held on to Speedy, the tenderness flooding over his face, as the child called out, "No go, no go"? Or had it been that moment when he had appeared in the doorway of her bedroom, strong and capable and ready to make love to her? Her heart sank whenever she remembered that she had failed to tell him about her fateful call to Social Services. The conflicting emotions of burgeoning love and mounting anxiety were beginning to make her crazy.

She looked up at her boss and waved distractedly. "Oh, good morning, Lou."

Lou Collier, who was used to people jumping to attention when he came barging into an office, was clearly taken aback. "Hey, Maguire, are you all right?"

"Mmmmm," was all she said.

"Well, I've got bad news for you," he continued, eyeing her curiously.

Andie didn't even lift an eyebrow.

"Hey! Maguire!" Lou barked, waving his hand in front of her face. "Are you in there?"

"I'm here, Lou."

"Well, good." He looked dubious but plunged ahead. "I need you to do another rewrite. Fredonia isn't coming back on the show for at least six months. We've got to put her in traction, and—" He stopped when he realized that his words were having absolutely no effect on her.

"Oh, I'm sorry, Lou. Did you want something?"

Lou gave an exasperated sigh and threw up his hands. "What's going on around here? When I want results, I expect results." He scowled threateningly, but Andie met his bluff face with a sweet smile.

She had learned quickly that her boss's gruff manner

was only a front for a sensitive and insightful nature. It occurred to her that he might be able to sort out the complexities in her life. After all, he was a man, and right now getting a man's opinion seemed like a very good idea. "Say, Lou," she ventured. "Can I ask you something?"

"If it's about a raise—"

"Oh, no, no," she assured him. "It's nothing like that. It's just that—" She took a deep breath. "Can I confide in you?"

Collier looked suspicious. "You want to confide in me?"

"Why not?"

"Nobody ever confides in me around here," he said. "It wouldn't be proper—or smart. And do you know why?"

Andie shook her head, her green eyes luminous with interest.

Lou paused for a second in spite of himself, but then pressed on. "It's because I'm the boss, that's why. People are supposed to hide things from me, not confide in me. That's how we get things done." He looked at her shrewdly, continuing with deliberate exaggeration. "That allows me to yell at people and get angry. If they started *confiding* in me, I would feel obligated to be *nice* to them."

Andie looked so crestfallen that he scowled even harder. He turned for a moment as if he were going to leave, swung back in frustration and hit a fist on the desk, and finally fell into a chair. "Okay, okay, what is it? Make it quick."

Andie gave him a wan smile. "I don't even know how to begin." She hesitated.

"Try English," he quipped.

She took a deep breath and told him the entire story of George and Speedy, leaving nothing out. Lou listened with a slight frown, as if trying to absorb it all, but she had the comforting feeling that he was taking her seriously.

"So here I am," she finished, "with a hectic job, crazy neighbors, a two-year-old child with an absent mother who could show up at any time, and a guy who stores his TV dinners in alphabetical order. And to make matters worse, George doesn't know I made that call to Social Services. He'll *kill* me when he finds out, and I just don't have the nerve to tell him." She fell back in her chair and looked up at him appealingly. "So if I'm preoccupied, you can see I've got plenty of reason."

Lou looked her up and down and gave a short burst of laughter. "You know something? If this were a plot from a soap, I'd throw it out for being too unbelievable."

"What do you mean?" she asked rather crossly. She had expected sympathy, not criticism.

Collier held up a finger. "First, the situation with the kid is too far-fetched. No one takes a child for an hour and then ends up baby-sitting for nearly three weeks."

"George did."

"Two," Lou continued, ignoring her remark, "we could never use a character like this George. He's simply too eccentric."

Andie blinked in surprise. She was used to George by now. To her, he no longer seemed eccentric, but endearing.

"He's too idiosyncratic," Lou insisted. "Our audience would never go for a character like that. We look for someone our viewers can identify with and fall in love with. Someone they might know. Who the hell could fall in love with a guy like this?"

"I did," Andie informed him weakly.

Lou started for a moment, but took her revelation in stride. "Well, then, you've got a problem, kid," he said sternly. "I've seen too many plots like this turn sour."

"It's not a plot," she said helplessly. "It's my life."

"Are you asking my advice?" She nodded. "Fair enough. Don't say I didn't warn you. You've got to tell him you called Social Services, and tell him why," he said. "You called them behind the guy's back. That wasn't fair. He's bound to be unpleasantly surprised when he finds out. My suggestion is that you tell him yourself, and do it fast before they pay him a surprise visit."

Andie sighed and looked at her lap. Lou was right, of course. She had been stalling on asking anyone for advice because she knew, deep down, that they'd tell her to level with George. She realized that she'd avoided telling him because she didn't want anything to interfere with their budding relationship. It had been too special, and she had wanted to reserve it for as long as she could before deliberately throwing in a thorn.

Collier gave her a curious little smile. "You can't have it both ways," he said quietly, seeming to read her mind. "You can't inform on the guy and then expect him to love you at the same time." She nodded, lost in thought.

"And that's enough advice for the lovelorn," he said decisively. "I told you, I don't like to be Mr. Nice Guy." Andie hid a smile. "I need a rewrite on that hospital scene," he went on, summoning his usual gruffness. "How soon can you have it?"

"A couple of hours," she answered.

Lou played with that a second. "Have it on my desk before noon," he ordered. "Then take the rest of the day off."

Her face lit up with gratitude. "Oh, thank you, Lou. That's really—"

"No, it's not," he cut in. "Don't tell me I'm nice. I

can't handle it. I just don't want to see your personal life infiltrating this office, is that clear?"

Andie nodded eagerly, trying to look chastened.

"Good." He stood up and stalked out. Andie sank back and indulged in a fit of giggles that ended abruptly when she realized that she now had to face George with the truth.

George was surprised to see Andie at his door an hour later, but he welcomed her with a kiss that made her heart jump.

"I was expecting a new file cabinet to be delivered," he murmured as his hands ran possessively down the sides of her body, "but this is much better."

She picked up a large shopping bag she had left on the floor in the hall. "I brought lunch," she announced, marching inside just in time to prevent Speedy from tipping over a half-filled coffee cup. "I have the whole afternoon off."

He took the bag into the kitchen. "So what's the occasion?" he asked. "You never get home early."

Panic gripped her. She couldn't tell him yet—not so soon, not just after she had walked in the door. She improvised quickly. "It's our anniversary today," she gulped. "We've been going steady for two whole weeks."

"Has it been that long?" George quipped. "My, my, how time flies."

Andie sat down nervously. She groped for the opening words to the sensible speech she had prepared on the way over, but it deserted her as she looked at him. "George," she began, "I—that is, we—there's something—" She took a deep breath to steady herself and plunged ahead. "I have something important to talk over with you, and it can't wait."

He sat down next to her, apparently affected by her serious tone. "Sure, honey, what's the matter?"

His concern melted her. She swallowed and looked down, her fingers playing with the material of her skirt. "Things have been ... different in your life lately— haven't they?" she asked. "I mean—" She stopped, praying for the right words.

"Do you need help?" George asked with a little smile. "Because I have a feeling I know what you're going to ask."

"You do?"

He nodded.

"No, you don't," Andie concluded miserably after looking into his eyes. He looked so handsome and strong, and her heart swelled. Why did she have to be so in love with him?

"Oh, but I do," George insisted, taking her chin in his hand. He looked deeply into her eyes, captivating her completely. "Ever since we met, Andie, my life has changed enormously."

"But—but what about Speedy?" she managed to choke out. "Don't you think he had something to do with your life changing?"

He smiled with supreme confidence. "Speedy was here before you were. I'm not talking about him now. I'm talking about you and me."

"Oh." He had no idea how wretched she was feeling at that moment, and how utterly torn in two directions. How she wanted to pour her heart out to him, to tell him how much she had come to love him. But the question of Speedy's future, and what she had done about it, loomed before her.

He bent and kissed her gently. "Happy anniversary."

"What?" she asked distractedly. "Oh—no, I don't

think so." He sat back, surprised but amused, obviously confident that no problem could be great enough to stop the inevitable. She turned her head and he caught her chin, turning her to face him.

"What is it?" he asked.

Suddenly, the doorbell rang.

"That must be my file cabinet," he said reluctantly. "I'll be right with you." He got up and buzzed the downstairs front door, listening as it opened and someone entered the building.

The sudden quiet jarred Andie into a realization: Where was Speedy? She looked around. "Hey, Speedy? Where are you?" She glanced toward the kitchen and caught sight of the little boy as he climbed deftly into the old dumbwaiter. "That's your favorite hiding place, isn't it?" She stood up as he seated himself comfortably inside, clutching his worn teddy bear.

"I got Teddy," he announced seriously.

"Sorry, Speedy, but you can't play in there." Shaking her head, she started over to retrieve him when she suddenly perceived a barely noticeable movement on the old pulleys. She stopped for a second and blinked her eyes to make sure it wasn't her imagination. Sure enough, the ropes moved again, but now the motion was more pronounced. Her heart in her mouth, she made a lunge for Speedy just as he yanked on the ropes.

At that moment, George turned and stepped back. "He's at it again," he said, unaware of the danger.

Andie crashed into him, her lunge broken by his sudden interference. "Quick!" she cried. "Get him!"

"Oh, my God," George exclaimed, turning, but it was too late.

Speedy's grubby hands gave a decisive tug, and the dumbwaiter jerked up, disappearing behind the wall.

"Speedy!" Andie screamed. George threw himself at the opening, reaching up.

"Wheeee!" Speedy's little voice trailed an echo down into the heart of the building as George groped frantically to reach him.

"It's heading for my apartment," Andie said in alarm. She was out the door and taking the stairs three at a time, her keys already in the lock and turning by the time she banged her door open. George was right behind her, racing toward the dumbwaiter shaft and tearing the door open. They could hear Speedy in back of it.

"It's stuck!" George yelled. "Get me a screwdriver!"

She grabbed one from a kitchen drawer and tossed it to him, her heart pounding. "Hold on, Speedy," he called, going to work on the door. "I'm coming to get you." The door wouldn't budge and he prepared for a massive effort. "Stand back!" he commanded. "One—two—three!" With one powerful surge, he tore the door from its hinges, falling backward in the process to land on the floor.

They looked up warily and saw Speedy sitting calmly in the dumbwaiter, which bounced uneasily with his every move. His little fists were playing with the ropes, and they sensed that any sudden movement would propel him into pulling on them.

"Get him, George!" Andie exclaimed as he scrambled over to retrieve the child.

"I will," George vowed, inching forward. "I just don't want to scare him. Don't move."

Speedy smiled sweetly, still hanging on to the ropes and gazing at them innocently. He looked up with interest as George made his approach. Suddenly, a loud shout from down below made him jump in alarm. "Hello, up there! Anybody home?"

Andie turned, disconcerted, and saw a thin, earnest young man in a gray plaid suit standing on the landing. "Hi," he said in a nasal voice. "Is this Demarest Consultants?"

"Shh!" she hissed. "We have an emergency here."

The man looked up in time to see George carefully reaching for the child in the dumbwaiter. The mechanism bounced slowly up and down, making Andie hold her breath.

"Oh, my God!" the man yelled.

That did it. Speedy reacted to the excitement by giggling wildly and tugging at the ropes. In a moment, he was once again out of sight. "Bye-bye," they could hear his little voice calling in the shaft.

George lunged and grasped only air.

"The roof!" Andie shouted, and turned to bolt.

"No," the stranger said, pointing back at the shaft. "Look." They watched helplessly as Speedy passed by their eyes on his way down to the next level.

"Bye-bye," he said, laughing.

They all dashed for the door, heading back down to George's apartment. But by the time they got there, Speedy had already passed it.

"Is Sheila home?" Andie asked as they raced down the next flight of stairs.

"If she's not, I'll break down her door," George said, brandishing the screwdriver in his hand.

But she was there. Clad in a flowing tie-dyed caftan, Sheila greeted them mournfully at her door.

"You caught me in the midst of my finding my third eye," she informed them.

George was not interested. "Out of my way," he said frantically, shoving her aside in his battle to get to the dumbwaiter. Unfortunately, the door to the dumbwaiter was covered by a picture of Sheila's guru. George tore it from the wall without ado, and Sheila railed at him, aghast.

"That's my Maharishi," she cried out. "What do you think you're doing?"

"There's a baby stuck in the wall behind him," Andie tried to explain.

Sheila stared at her, uncomprehending. "A baby?"

Andie nodded and looked around for a tool to help George get the door open, but saw nothing that looked remotely useful. The place was smoky with incense and was decorated from wall to wall with faded Indian bedspreads.

"Do you have a hammer?" she asked Sheila, who was still bewildered.

"A baby?" Sheila muttered. "I knew my karma was going to be strange today."

"Forget the hammer," George yelled. "I've almost got it." He was frantically clawing away at the edges of the door. "It's been painted shut, but—" Suddenly, he gave it a sharp pull.

The door flew open, but all they could see were the ropes moving slowly from an unseen force. The stranger stepped forward authoritatively, brushing past George to stick his head inside the shaft and look down. "I can't see a thing," he said. "It's too dark."

Unfortunately, he should have looked up. In the next instant, the dumbwaiter came down on his head. "Ouch!" he yelled.

George reached out and grabbed him by his belt, pulling him out of danger. They both lost their balance and fell backward, watching helplessly as Speedy calmly sailed by them.

Speedy waved companionably as the dumbwaiter descended to the next floor.

"A baby," Sheila said solemnly. "It really was a baby. Behind the Maharishi."

George lit a match and peered down the dusty shaft. "I can see the dumbwaiter," he said as the rope continued to move. "It's past the Hernandez's place."

He studied the rope for a moment and blew out the match, looking at Andie with sudden confidence. "Why didn't I think of it before?" he asked, his face lit with a new idea. And waving them all back, he began to pull gently on the rope to slow it down. "It's stopping," he said tensely as a cloud of dust from the old rope began to swirl off his hands. He coughed, and the stranger stepped forward curiously.

"Pull," George commanded him. "Come on, help me."

The stranger obligingly grabbed the rope, and the two men pulled in unison. "It's moving!" George shouted.

The man coughed. "I'm allergic to dust," he explained.

"Pull!" George insisted.

"I'm pulling, I'm pulling."

By now both their faces were splotched with soot, and Sheila's red carpet was a mess.

"I've got a mantra meeting this Saturday night," she moaned, shaking her head. "They'll never believe this."

"Pull!" Andie urged, ignoring Sheila. "Pull!"

"I think I see it," George said. "Yes, that's it. Keep pulling—it's almost here."

Andie ran over and stood next to them, ready to grab Speedy. But when the dumbwaiter finally arrived, they were dismayed to see that it was empty.

"Oh, no!" Andie cried. "He must have gotten out in the basement."

Without another word, they all rushed out of Sheila's apartment and down the stairs.

"Watch out for that bicycle!" Andie warned, but no one heard her in the frenzy. George tripped first and was followed by the stranger, whose hands flew up unwittingly to catch her as she fell. She scrambled hastily out of his arms and stood up, finding herself at the bottom of the steps in front of the basement apartment.

George was still on the floor as the door to the apartment opened. They looked up and saw a tall, somber man in a bathrobe, carrying Speedy in his arms. Speedy was laughing merrily, as if they had all been playing a game devised especially for his amusement.

The man surveyed the hapless trio stiffly. "I believe this belongs to one of you," he said formally.

"I'll take him," George said, standing up and brushing himself off.

The man placed Speedy in George's arms. "Thank you," George said. "Mr.—uh—" He stopped, confused, but Andie filled in for him.

"You're Barnes, right?" It was almost like seeing a ghost.

The man nodded, as if they should have known. "Of course. And now, if you will excuse me, I have to get back to sleep."

They watched as he disappeared inside and shut the door.

"So that's Barnes," George mused. He looked at Speedy for a long time and shook his head. "Well, Speedy, I guess you think I'm very irresponsible."

"It's my fault, too, George," Andie broke in. "I should have moved faster."

"No," George insisted. "It's all my fault. I should

have checked to make sure that dumbwaiter was safe before using it as a closet. I'm supposed to be an efficiency expert. I should think of things like that."

Andie was stricken by the dismay on his face. "Don't be so hard on yourself, George. You've been trying to do the impossible. No one can run a business and take care of a two-year-old—not without help. You try to do everything yourself, and this is what happens. You have no experience with this sort of thing. It was inevitable that Speedy would have an accident. We were lucky this time."

"But what about the next time?" George pressed, determined to have it out. "Let's face it, I'm not fit to take care of him."

Andie wanted to console him, but the scare they had just had sobered her. "Neither am I," she added finally. "We're not cutting it, George."

"I'm a bachelor, not a homemaker. My whole apartment is no environment for Speedy. In fact, it's a danger zone. I've set up my life to function around me, not me and a child."

Andie was nodding miserably, when the stranger coughed.

"Ah—ahem."

"Oh, I'm terribly sorry," George said, looking up. "You have a delivery for me?"

"Delivery?" The man shook his head wearily. "No, I have no delivery. I'm Morty Carlson," he said as he dusted himself off and wiped his face with a handkerchief. "Call me Morty."

"Oh. Well, thank you for your help, Morty," George said, extending a hand. "I'm happy to have made your acquaintance."

"Oh, I don't think so," Morty said dryly, ignoring the

proferred hand. "Especially after the conversation I just overheard."

Andie and George stared at him, bewildered.

"I'm not a delivery man, as you seemed to assume," he explained smugly, taking out a business card and slapping it into George's palm. "I'm from Social Services."

Chapter Nine

GEORGE STOOD LIKE a statue next to the mantel of his apartment for the whole two hours that Morty Carlson conducted his preliminary investigation. He never moved once, not even when the Social Services investigator asked a question or made a point. Every time Andie tried to intervene, George cut her off abruptly or ignored her altogether.

Speedy lay quietly in the next room, blissfully unaware that his future was being charted as he slept. When the interview was just about over, Morty got up and tiptoed over to the doorway of the bedroom to get a glimpse of the child. Shaking his head, he jotted something down on his clipboard.

"Try putting some pillows around him so he won't fall out," he suggested. "We wouldn't want Joshua to roll off the bed to the floor."

George said nothing, but his eyes shot daggers at Andie.

"Uh—that's my fault," Andie said hastily. "I put Speedy to bed, and . . . " Her voice trailed. "Sorry," she finished lamely.

Morty wrote something else down, and turned his attention back to George. "I'll need a picture of your cousin Mindy," he said. "Also an affidavit from your lawyer, proving your relationship to Joshua."

"You'll have it on your desk tomorrow morning at nine o'clock sharp."

"Is there anything I can do?" Andie asked sheepishly.

George looked at her for a split second, but his flinty gaze seemed to go right through her. She stifled a sigh, sure that Morty could sense the hostility.

"No, Ms. Maguire," he answered formally. "This is strictly a family matter, and it must remain so. Mr. Demarest is, as far as we know, the closest living relative. That will suffice—for the moment."

"So what happens now?" George asked abruptly.

Morty raised an eyebrow and coughed delicately. "Well, let's see." He looked over his notes and gave them a thin smile. "First we'll try and find the mother. You can keep Speedy for now. But a determination will be made later after your cousin has been located."

"And that's up to you, isn't it?" George asked grimly.

"Oh, no," Morty said. "It's a lot more complicated than just a few notes."

Andie spoke up. "And what if Mindy can't be found?"

"Yes," George said without looking at her. "Does that mean I can adopt Speedy?"

Morty took a deep breath, as if he'd been through this a million times before. "It's tricky," he said. "The laws are funny about these things."

"How so?" George asked impatiently.

"Domesticity is a very important factor in—I mean,

the amount of time a parent spends with a child—" Morty took another breath and gave it to him straight. "If you were a woman, it would be easier."

"But that's not fair!" Andie cried. "That's the most ridiculous double standard I ever heard."

"Maybe so," Morty said primly, "but also the way of the world, at least for now. I'm not giving you my personal opinion," he added. "I'm just telling you what kind of thinking to expect." He looked at both of them, tallying their reactions. "Well," he said, standing up, "I must be going." He started for the door but turned back, his face softening a little. "May I make a suggestion?"

George's face was a stone mask. "Please do."

"This apartment," Morty said. "It needs some work to become a proper environment for a two-year-old." He flipped through the pages of his clipboard. Removing a pamphlet, he handed it to George. "This will help you to childproof so that accidents such as the unfortunate one we had a few hours ago won't recur. I also suggest that you empty your medicine cabinet of any dangerous pills and razor blades," he added. "If Joshua can climb into a dumbwaiter, he certainly can scale a bathroom sink to reach the medicine chest."

George nodded, and Morty held out his hand. "Good day to you both," he said. There was a short pause. Then George shook Morty's hand and held the door open as the social worker stepped out.

There was a long silence as they sat listening to Morty's diminishing footsteps. Andie looked at the floor until she could hear the front door closing. When she looked up, she saw that George was still holding the door open.

"Phew," she said. "That was tough, huh?"

George said nothing.

"Please don't look at me that way, George."

He didn't say a word.

"Look, I know you have a right to be angry, but if you'll just listen, I can explain."

"Get out!" he said sternly, still holding the door open.

Andie was startled, but she held her ground. "Please, George, I only meant to help."

"Out!" He repeated the command bitingly, and there was no mistaking his fury. "Now!"

Tears welled in her eyes, tears of frustration as well as sadness. She had never seen George like this, and she barely knew what to say. "I know I did it behind your back," she pleaded, "but I was thinking of you as well as Speedy."

He remained unmoved. "I don't want to hear it," he snapped. He jerked his thumb toward the door. "I'm waiting."

She stood up and walked toward the door, trying desperately to maintain her poise. The moment she was outside, the door slammed behind her, leaving a chilling silence. She ran up to her apartment and threw herself on her bed, dissolving into tears.

That was the last she saw of George. The rest of the day was spent in on-and-off-again tears and self-criticism. After calming down somewhat by evening, she tried calling him, but all she got was his answering machine. Giving up hope for a quick reconciliation, she dragged herself to work the next morning and spent the rest of the day lost in the doldrums. By three o'clock, she hadn't accomplished a thing except to feel even more miserable. Resting her head on the desk, she thought about George's angry face once again and let two large tears roll down her cheeks.

Lou Collier chose this inauspicious moment to barge

into her office. "Hey, Maguire!" He threw a script down on her desk. "That stuff you wrote this morning stinks."

Andie looked up at him, her face still wet with tears.

"Aw, now," he retreated, reacting awkwardly to her emotion. "You don't have to cry over it. I know you can do better. After all, last week's script was terrific." He grabbed a few tissues from her Kleenex box and handed them to her.

"Thank you, Lou," she said, mustering enough dignity to dab at her face. "I'm not crying over criticism, at least not yours."

Collier seemed disappointed. "Oh, yeah? Jeez, and I thought I was doing good." He folded his arms roughly and sat on the edge of her desk. "Don't tell me that efficiency character of yours is still giving you a hard time."

She nodded sadly.

"You blew it, didn't you?" he concluded. "I should have known. What happened, he found out you squealed before you could tell him yourself?" Another miserable nod. "Yeah, that's what I figured."

Andie was hopeful. At least Lou wasn't bawling her out, and maybe he could offer some good advice. "So what do I do now?" she sniffed.

"You still want *my* advice?"

"Sure, why not? I can use all the help I can get."

She waited eagerly while Lou rubbed his chin with one finger. After a moment, his face lit up and he pointed down at Andie. "You know what your problem is?" he demanded.

She shook her head. "No, what?"

"Your problem is you're all upset over this. *He's* the one who should be upset."

"Oh, he is, believe me."

"What I mean is, you've got nothing to apologize for. Stop crying already. You only did what you thought was right. He's being too hard on you. Let *him* come and apologize to *you*."

Andie let out a long, shaky sigh. "I don't know, Lou. I don't think he'll come at all. I may have gone too far for that."

"Yeah, well, then you have to make it happen. You have to create the circumstance that leads him to you."

"And how do I do that?"

Lou smiled. "You're the writer. Go figure it out. I just give the orders, remember?"

By the time she got home, she had created six different excuses for seeing George, all of them rotten. Going down to borrow a cup of sugar was corny, pretending to be the Avon lady was stupid, and enticing him with a homemade pecan pie was more trouble than it was worth, since it probably wouldn't work anyway. The other three were too drastic to even think about. There was nothing to do but sit curled up in an armchair and wait for something to happen. A half hour later, something did.

Oblivious of time, she was contemplating a peanut-butter-and-jelly sandwich for dinner when the doorbell suddenly rang.

"George!" she said aloud, running over to answer it. Mr. Collier was right, she thought. He was coming to apologize. But instead of George, it was a burly man with a huge box.

"Excuse me, ma'am, but I got this delivery here for a Mr. George Demarest—only he ain't home."

Andie looked beyond the man and down the stairs, where two other men waited with a large box.

"If you wouldn't mind?" He held out a paper for her signature.

"Oh, I guess I can sign for it." Without looking at what she was signing, Andie took the pen and scribbled her name on the dotted line. But she wasn't prepared for what she had just orchestrated.

"Okay, guys," the man shouted. "Bring it all up."

"Up?" she asked. "Oh, you mean you have to leave it in my apartment?"

"If you don't mind. It's for safekeeping."

Fifteen minutes later, her living room looked as if she had just moved in all over again. Boxes were stacked everywhere, some of them larger than her own furniture.

Curious, she picked up the delivery slip and read it. "Baby World," she said aloud, and went down all the items, checking them off as they were deposited in her apartment. There was everything from a small bed and a dresser to a high chair, an indoor child's swing, and even a rocking horse. Along with all of that came a month's supply of diapers, oil, powder, cotton balls, and even a manual on child care, which the man placed right into Andie's hands.

Well, at least now she had an excuse to see George again, she thought hopefully. Maybe by now he had cooled down somewhat. But when she bravely went down the stairs later that night after hearing him come in, she was sorely disappointed.

"Hello," she called in cautiously. "George? It's me, Andie. Are you there?"

It took a moment for him to respond. "I'm here," an angry voice finally answered from the other side of the door.

There was an awkward pause. "Uh, George?" Andie tried again. "Could we talk?"

"What do you call what we're doing now?"

"Can't we talk face-to-face?"

The door unhinged and opened slowly to reveal George looking utterly disheveled. He had a screwdriver in his hand and behind him lay more unopened cartons of all sizes. His entire living room was a shambles of sawdust and tools, and all his furniture was pushed into a corner, covered by sheets. She saw that his bedroom door was closed and surmised that Speedy was inside, sleeping on George's bed.

"I'm putting up some shelves," he explained in response to her puzzled glare. "They have to be high enough to keep Speedy from reaching them." He glanced at the guidelines Morty Carlson had given him. "Five feet high, and away from anything that can be climbed on," he read.

Andie looked back at his living room wall, where the mirror had hung. There was a series of holes drilled in the wall, and a half dozen wooden shelves were leaning against it.

"What do you think?" George asked, apparently still reluctant to make conversation but too curious for an opinion to refuse to talk to her. "Is that high enough to pass inspection?"

"Inspection?" Andie asked weakly.

"Yes, inspection. Ever since you informed on me, I've been out trying to get everything I need to qualify as a temporary guardian. I don't have much time, either. According to your friend Morty, they can barge into my private domain at any time and surprise me." He looked at her furiously, his anger mounting once again, and began to close the door. "Now, if you don't mind, I'm busy."

But Andie wasn't ready to be thrown out. Not this time. A glimmer of anger stole into her misery, and she was glad of it. It was certainly a welcome relief from all

that useless guilt. "I could help, you know," she informed
George icily.

"I don't want your help."

That did it. Something inside Andie snapped, and she
barged past him into his apartment. Putting her hands on
her hips, she gave George a withering once-over. "Now
you listen to me, you stubborn mule. I may have been
a buttinsky by making that call to Social Services, but
you're not handling it well at all. I'm going to help you,
whether you like it or not."

And with that, she headed over to the far wall, knocking over the shelves that were resting against it. It made
a loud bang, and she and George stood stock-still, praying that Speedy wouldn't wake up.

After several long moments that felt like an eternity,
Andie breathed a sigh of relief. "Phew," she said, giving
him a baleful look. "That was close, huh?"

George merely scowled.

"Look, I'm sorry," she said.

"Out, now." He held the door open.

Andie threw her arms out in frustration. "Are you
going to keep throwing me out all the time? Because if
you are, I'd like to know now. Otherwise, you'd better
start being more hospitable."

"Out!"

She simply wasn't going to allow this. It wasn't fair
to her. Besides, she didn't think she could endure another
horrible day alone in her apartment. She had to do something or she would go crazy. She stole a glance at him
and saw that he still looked perfectly immovable. But
she couldn't believe that he really meant to throw her
out of his life. "You just need to go outside for a walk,
George," she suggested. "I'll stay here and put up these
shelves, and when you've calmed down enough, you can

come back and we'll talk, okay?"

She picked up a screwdriver as if the matter were settled and scooped up some screws. Heading over to the far wall, she began to go through the motions of measuring the spaces for the brackets, all too aware that George hadn't moved.

"Go on," she said after an unendurable silence.

But George just stood there glaring at her, his eyes sending darts of anger across the room that were almost palpable.

"You are a very stubborn man, George Demarest," Andie said to the wall. Finally, she couldn't take it any longer. She threw the screwdriver on the floor and faced him. "If I leave now, George, don't count on my coming back." In her heart, she knew that she was lying through her teeth, but at that moment she almost wished she could mean what she was saying. It took two to make a relationship work, and George was not meeting her halfway. "May I just ask one thing of you?" she continued coldly.

"What is it?"

"Would you please go upstairs and get those things that Baby World delivered? They're scattered all over my apartment."

She expected an equally icy response, but this news made George's face light up. "It arrived? The new furniture? Why didn't you tell me? I've been waiting hours for it."

"Well, it's all there," she said.

George ran out and up the stairs, letting the door shut behind him. She listened speculatively as he reached the upper landing and tried her door. It was locked. A slow smirk crossed her face as George ran back down the stairs and rapped lightly on his own door. "Hey, Andie," he whispered loudly. "I'll need the keys to your apartment. Your door is locked."

"I know that, George," Andie whispered back.

"So let's have them." He rattled the door. "Open up."

"Use your keys," she said with a smile. "I'm busy."

"But I don't have my keys with me! I can't get in!"

The smile spread across her face, becoming a smug grin. "How convenient," she said with mock sweetness. "I'll see you later. Your nice long walk starts right now."

"You tricked me!" he shouted, rattling futilely at the door.

"You tricked yourself. Now get going, and don't come back until you've turned back into a rational human being. If you can't manage rational, at least try for calm enough to attempt normal communication. It's more *efficient* that way."

Something resembling a growl emanated from the other side of the door, and then Andie listened in satisfaction as his footsteps vanished down the stairs.

It was a good hour before he returned.

"Who's there?" Andie called with a straight face when he knocked on the door.

"Who do you think?"

"Are you sufficiently calmed down?"

"Most *e*fficiently," he answered.

"That will suffice." She opened the door, but the angry scowl was still there. She squinted at him in calculation. "You still look upset," she concluded, her heart dropping.

"Out," he said as he plowed through the door. "Right now."

Andie was dumbfounded. "You—you lied! You're not calmed down at all."

"All's fair in love and war," he stated. "And this is

definitely war." He looked critically around the apartment as if expecting her to have ruined or broken something during his absence. But his eyes fell on the shelves that she had put up, and he smiled in spite of himself. "Hey, look at that," he said. He went over and examined her handiwork. "Well, I'll be a monkey's uncle."

"Try son of a mule," Andie suggested, still smarting at his rude entrance.

He was impressed, no doubt about it. She could tell because the scowl had left his face, replaced by a sparkle in his eyes that she had despaired of seeing again. "You're full of surprises, aren't you?" He allowed her a pointed glance, one that seemed to reassess her, and went over to inspect the shelves more closely. Picking up a ruler, he made exact measurements. "Perfect," he pronounced, "right down to the centimeter."

"The top joint of my thumb is exactly one inch," she informed him, holding up her thumb.

There was a long silence, during which Andie waited breathlessly for him to break the ice. The look that passed between them reminded her irrationally of the one they had exchanged the very first day they had met, standing downstairs on the front stoop. It was a look of inevitability, of recognition. Her smile was radiant as she accepted the obvious.

George looked like a little boy caught in his own trap. He looked up, looked down, and finally ambled over to her, standing so close to her that her blood jumped.

"Do you have any idea the trouble you've cost me?" He answered that himself. "No, you don't. How could you?"

"Mistakes can be fixed," Andie said.

"Yes, they can, but with considerably more effort than it took to make them in the first place."

She could see that the barrier between them was finally starting to disintegrate. All they could do was look at each other and let their hidden feelings seep through the silence of that moment.

"I *was* thinking of you as well as Speedy when I called Social Services," she said, glad for the chance to set the record straight. To bolster her courage and to soften what she had to say next, she took his hand in hers. "I was convinced you were hiding your head in the sand, George. We were both play-acting at taking care of a child. Well, this isn't a game for Speedy. You were dashing around like a circus performer, trying to juggle and balance your act. Speedy doesn't need an act. He needs stability. And he needs more than just a roof over his head." She finished her long speech, unaware that her hand was gripping his tightly.

George looked down and said nothing for a long moment. But his hand remained locked in hers, and when he spoke, his voice was intently earnest. "I don't think you know how much Speedy means to me, Andie. Okay, maybe I made some mistakes at the beginning. But I feel an attachment to him that transcends a lot of other things. I was adopted myself, you know."

She searched his face, moved by the conviction she saw there. "I guess you do know what it's like." She nodded sympathetically.

George shook his head. "No, don't get melodramatic on me again. I told you, I had a perfectly happy childhood. But I'm aware of the breadth of the responsibility I want to take on."

Comprehension dawned on her face. "Are you telling me . . . Do you mean that you want to keep Speedy— permanently?"

"Of course," he said with a trace of his old impatience.

"What do you think this is all about?"

"But you never said—I thought you just wanted to take care of him until Mindy can be located."

"Don't be ridiculous. Now who's hiding her head in the sand? Face reality, Andie. Mindy isn't fit to take care of him. She never was. Do you think I'm going to let them hand that child back to *her?*"

Andie digested this slowly, fitting all the pieces together. Her heart sank as she recalled the episode with the dumbwaiter and Morty Carlson's glum face as he surveyed the situation. "I'm so sorry, George," she whispered, tears springing to her eyes. "I wish you had told me."

"It's not time to worry yet," he reassured her. "I've got everything under control."

"You would," she said with a glimmer of a smile, glad that the rapport between them was back. "If it will help any, I'll call Morty Carlson and tell him to withhold the Last Judgment until he has his facts straight. Then you and I will do a job on this place and turn it into the best environment for a two-year-old in town." Her eyes flashed with a new idea. "And I could check out a nursery school for him. There's a terrific one over on Seventy-eighth Street, run by two very no-nonsense English ladies. They take sixteen kids a year and the place is toddler's paradise."

"How do you know all this?" George asked.

"Oh—well, I sort of stopped in and asked. I was just . . . curious," she stammered.

"Curious or something more?"

She looked at him, puzzled, waiting for an explanation. All of a sudden, it seemed as if George knew something she didn't.

"You're something else, you know that?" he murmured, his golden-brown eyes caressing her. Her hands touched his arms tentatively, and the simple touch brought them together in a sudden jolt of electricity.

"Oh, George, I really am sorry. I truly did mean well."

"Shhhh," he whispered. "It will all work itself out with a little help from us."

She looked up into his eyes. "Us?"

He smiled at her and nodded, and the dam broke. All at once she was lost in his arms, their mouths joining in a thankful rush of relief. George kissed her again and again and again, sealing their truce and stroking her hair with a tenderness that thrilled her.

Now she knew more than ever what she wanted, needed. Lou had been half right, she realized as George swept her into a whirlwind of pleasure. George would have to come to her, all right, but not with an apology. Now she wanted much more from him than that—and she wanted it to last much longer than one fleeting night.

Chapter Ten

IT SEEMED NATURAL and right for them to spend the
night together. For Andie, it was all simple and clear.
Her love for George was singing and shouting from every
pore in her body. She was sure he must be able to tell
how she felt. They were so perfect when they were together like this, all their differences suddenly blending
and fitting like pieces of a puzzle.

And yet she became inexplicably shy when faced with
the dim light of morning. George was so self-sufficient
and unpredictable. She couldn't summon the courage to
tell him how she felt, and now she was no longer sure
he knew. George always seemed to know everything he
wanted to know—and this was something he didn't necessarily want at all. A night of passion was hardly the
answer to weeks of unanswered questions.

There wasn't much time to think about it. Andie had
to race upstairs to her own apartment to get dressed for
work. The subject of George and Speedy was on her

mind all day, and she rushed home as soon as she could, anxious to see George and to unravel the confusion that enveloped her.

But when she knocked on his door after running up the stairs, there was no answer. Disappointed, she climbed the last flight to her own apartment, and was disconcerted to find a neatly typed note taped to her door. "They found Mindy," it said. "She's in Los Angeles. I'm flying out there immediately. I'll call you when I get back. Love, George."

That was all. There wasn't even a phone number. Dumbstruck, Andie opened her door and reread the note, trying to make sense out of it. Was George going out there to bring Mindy back? Or to drop Speedy off?

The thought of Speedy being left in California enraged her suddenly, and she couldn't figure out why. Speedy belonged here, with George—and, she realized with a sinking heart, with her. How could she have been so blind? The ingenuous two-year-old wasn't just any cute kid to her. He had carved himself a place in her heart, and the thought of losing him was suddenly devastating.

No wonder George had been so angry with her for calling Social Services! She hadn't just usurped his position and taken the upper hand—she had seriously threatened George's chances for becoming the full-time parent he obviously wanted to be. She plunked down on a chair and hit herself on the head with her palm. "Idiot!" she said aloud.

It occurred to her to call Morty Carlson at Social Services, but, she decided wretchedly, that would only increase the trouble she had caused. There was nothing she could do now but wait. She sat night after night in her apartment, listening for sounds of George's return.

By the middle of the following week, she could bear

it no more. It was Wednesday evening and she was a total wreck, sitting morosely in front of the television, watching *Family Feud*. Her mind kept returning to the wonderful times she had had with George, going over and over them, down to every last detail. How had she managed to intertwine her life so completely with his? Worse, how had she managed to fall in love with him in such a short time? She thought back to the first time she had seen him, looking so competent and handsome that day on the front stoop. Her heart had been touched even then, she admitted grimly. The way he had devoted himself without question to Speedy had made a deep impression on her. Any man who would commit to taking care of a two-year-old who had been dumped on him was a giant in her book. She knew that now.

"I am a hopeless case," she muttered as a commercial for floor wax came on. "This can't go on." She seriously debated the idea of picking up the phone and calling every hotel in Los Angeles, but that was crazy. She sighed defeatedly and turned her attention back to the game show.

The doorbell rang. Without thinking, she turned down the television and threw on an old, ratty bathrobe. "Who is it?"

"Me."

Her heart stopped. "George! I don't believe it! Oh— wait a minute!" She panicked. How could she let him see her like this? She looked like an unmade bed.

"Open up, I've got something I want to talk to you about."

She looked around wildly. Finally, she picked up a hairbrush and ran it madly through her hair. Then she threw it down and reached for the nearest cosmetic, a bottle of spray cologne. The mechanism didn't work properly, and she ended up dousing her knees with *L'Air du Temps*.

"Andie?" George called to her. "Come on, open up."

She opened the door excitedly. There he was, looking so dear and familiar that she wanted to throw herself into his arms and stay there. Speedy was perched in one arm, and his little face lit up when he saw her. A dozen roses were balanced in George's other arm, and her heart surged with happiness.

"Everything is fine now," he announced before she could say a word. "Social Services says Speedy can continue to stay with me."

She was speechless. "What about Mindy? Was she in Los Angeles? What happened? God, George, you could at least have called." She looked from the roses to Speedy to George's beaming face. "When did you get back?"

"This morning. And don't start nagging yet," he said with good humor. "Here," he added, holding out the roses. "These are for you."

"Andie!" Speedy cried in his chirpy little voice. He reached out for her to take him, and she did, closing her eyes as she clasped the warm little body against hers. He remembered her. He remembered her name. Speedy hugged back with all his might.

"I missed you, sweetie," she whispered, kissing his rosy face. "How've you been?"

"He's been fine," George answered, "and so have I. May we come in?"

"Of course." She stepped back hospitably, no longer caring that the place was a mess. Then she caught sight of the glint in George's eye, a glint she knew all too well. Putting Speedy down and placing the roses on a table, she faced him squarely. "What's up, George? Something's going on, isn't it?"

"What do you mean?" he asked innocently. "I came here to see you. Is there a law against that?"

"I know you, George. You have that conniving look in your eyes."

He looked wounded. "I don't know what you mean."

She said nothing, squinting at him suspiciously. "Everything is fine?" she queried, lifting an eyebrow. "Just like that? You run off to L.A. without a word, leaving me here to worry and wonder what on earth is going on. Now you show up, cool as a cucumber in a cabbage patch, and you expect me to act as if nothing unusual has happened?"

"Come on downstairs with me," he said smoothly, neatly avoiding her many questions. He turned and walked to the door, but Andie hesitated. "Come on, I won't bite."

"Let me just get dressed," she relented. There was no use quibbling. She wanted to see him too much. George took Speedy into the hall, and she climbed quickly into a pair of jeans and a T-shirt.

When she was ready, he led her down the stairs with a definite air of secrecy. Whatever he was hiding was about to be revealed in his apartment. Her curiosity rose as she followed him, stopping on the landing as he got out his keys.

"Cast your eyes on this," George announced grandly. His door opened slowly to reveal an astonishing sight.

The entire apartment had been transformed.

Andie was stunned. The couch and chairs were gone, replaced by a studio bed and the dresser from the bedroom. The windows were all barred, the dumbwaiter shaft had been sealed up, and the coffee table now had rubber bumper guards around the corners. A wooden gate was locked across the entrance to the kitchen, and another gate was stretched across the entrance to the bedroom.

George pointed wordlessly in that direction, and she stumbled toward the bedroom, too stunned to speak. Inside, she saw a small bed covered with a quilt and several stuffed animals, a toy chest stuffed with brand-new toys, a toy motorcycle, and a miniature table and chairs set. The entire room had been wallpapered in a whimsical pattern of sky-blue teddy bears holding red balloons against a white backdrop.

Andie spun around, trying to take it all in. Even the exposed electric sockets were now covered by plastic protectors. What had once been the dazzling showplace of a highly efficient bachelor was now a homey nest for a rambunctious two-year-old and one deeply caring adult.

Andie blinked in awe. "I don't believe it," she said. "When did you have time to do all this?"

"We started it before I left. The rest was done today. The wallpaper men just left an hour ago. Do you like it?"

"It's quite efficient," was all she could say.

"So you approve?"

"Obviously Social Services did. I guess Morty gave you a clean bill of approval."

"I passed with flying colors." George beamed. "Morty said I was a natural at fatherhood."

"But what about Mindy?" Andie asked, frowning. "Did you locate her?"

"Yes," George said tersely. "She's shacked up with a guy she met on the beach. She agreed that she's too young and unstable to take care of Speedy, and she's perfectly willing for him to stay with me until a final decision is made." He clapped his hands together, wanting to dismiss the subject. "Now, what should we do tonight?"

Now Andie was sure that something was up. "Did you talk to her yourself?"

He nodded reluctantly. "Yes, Morty recommended it. Speedy and I had just enough time to pack and get to the airport." He paused, hesitating to continue, but a sudden surge of excitement won out. "Morty said the rest is just a formality. He doesn't think there will be any obstacles to my adopting Speedy legally."

"That's terrific, George!" Andie grabbed his arm joyfully. "Now all your troubles are over." George said nothing, merely smiling patiently, and once again she had the nagging feeling that he was leaving something out. She groped for an opening. "So . . . where is Mindy? Is she . . . coming here?"

He shook his head. "No, she's staying where she is. She's already said good-bye to Speedy. She'll be visiting him once in a while, but that's it." He looked relieved, and yet he still seemed to be nervous about something.

She considered, watching him carefully. He had taken on a very big responsibility. Maybe she was asking too many questions. Maybe what he needed was a little encouragement.

"What do you say to a nice walk down Columbus Avenue?" he suggested. "We could stop for Italian pastry and cappuccino. Then maybe we could catch a movie or perhaps head over to Lincoln Center for a concert."

She smiled uncertainly. "Uh, George, aren't you forgetting something?" She indicated Speedy, who was nodding off on George's bed.

"That's all taken care of. Gail should be here in another ten minutes. I told her Speedy would already be asleep when she got here."

"I see." Andie nodded several times, digesting the full

range of his planning. "You're a sneak, George, you know that?"

"I know," he said cheerfully. "But that way we can get out without all that separation anxiety."

"No," she said, exasperated. "I didn't mean *us* being sneaky," Andie said. "I meant *you* planning all this without telling me. Do you know I've been a nervous wreck all week? Why didn't you at least call me?"

Ignoring her questions, he gazed down at the dozing Speedy. "Look at him." He carried the child into his new bedroom and placed him gently on the bed, covering him with the quilt.

Andie joined him, standing silently by his side. Together, they looked down at the sleeping child.

"I kept him up very late all week, arranging everything," he explained in a whisper. "He's exhausted and jet lagged. I doubt if even the Hernandezes could wake him up tonight."

Andie sighed. "George, when did you have time to plan this evening?"

"What does that matter? The important thing is that we can be together tonight. I have some things I want to talk over with you."

"What things?" She couldn't help it. The suspicion rose in her again.

"Good things." George smiled.

Andie twisted a lock of hair and angled her eyes toward his. "You're planning something, aren't you, George?"

He grinned at her and smiled devilishly. "Guilty as charged."

"But you won't tell me what it's about?"

"All in good time, all in good time. But first things first."

It was another twenty minutes before Gail arrived, giving Andie time to get properly dressed. She didn't blame George for wanting to celebrate his good fortune, but in the back of her mind was a persistent alarm that kept telling her something wasn't quite right. Well, she decided, as she surveyed in the mirror the dress she had purchased that first day at Bergdorf's, whatever it was, she'd hear about it tonight.

She wasted no time in asking him as soon as they were out of the house. "So what's the big surprise?" she asked as they strolled down the avenue, savoring their time alone together.

"All in good time," George repeated, putting his arm around her waist and pulling her close.

The air was warm, but there was a pleasant breeze that brought a trace of promise in the air. Andie's heart lifted and her doubts dwindled as she walked alongside him. She was supremely happy at this moment, and she decided not to let anything ruin it.

They stopped to look in the window of a travel agency, staring at the posters of faraway places. "Do you know what I first liked about you the day I met you?" he asked playfully.

She walked on ahead of him, stopping in front of a flower shop. "Let me guess. It was my southern accent, right?"

He laughed and nodded. "I love the way you talk," he said. He plucked a carnation from an outdoor bin and handed it to her with a swift but tender kiss.

After giving the shopkeeper a dollar, he took her hand and led her down the street. "Know what I first liked about you?" she asked.

"My complete and utter spontaneity, right?"

She laughed at him. "You have never been spontaneous in your life, George Demarest. Even if lightning were to strike, you'd make a split-second but highly efficient plan to sidestep it."

George stopped and clasped her in his arms, kissing the stuffing out of her. "Do you believe that this is spontaneous?" he asked, refusing to release her as he pressed a series of kisses over her face.

"No," she said, fighting to remain calm. "But you're definitely improving."

"Then let's try something drastically spontaneous," he said.

"Oh, no, George. This could be serious."

He dropped to one knee on the sidewalk, causing several passersby to stare at him.

"Andie Maguire, will you marry me?"

Embarrassed by his mock proposal, she looked around. "Oh, really, George. Stop it. Come on, get up."

He looked injured. "I'm perfectly serious, Andie. I am asking you to marry me. Surely that's nothing to scoff at."

She looked down at him, startled. "You're—serious? You are actually asking me to marry you? Here, in the middle of Columbus Avenue?" He nodded eagerly. "Well . . . I don't know what to say."

"Say yes."

"But we've only—I mean, you don't . . . " She tugged at his hand. "Would you please get up, George? We're starting to attract attention."

"No, we're not. This is New York, no one's looking."

She glared at him sternly. "Are you really serious? Do you really mean this?" Her gaze became clear and direct, demanding the truth.

"Yes." The one word was just as lucid, his eyes meeting hers frankly, without a quiver.

Andie's head began to spin and her heart lifted. She knew at that moment that there was only one reply she could give him. It didn't matter that there were so many questions left to be answered. Nothing mattered now except that the man she loved wanted to marry her, and she would be a fool to let him get away.

"Yes!" she cried, throwing her head back and laughing with delight.

"Yes?" He looked amazed but pleased, definitely pleased.

Andie pulled him to his feet and threw her arms around him, kissing him in a state of pure rapture. The emotion that had been building and yearning for release spilled out of her now; she no longer felt shy. "I love you, George Demarest!" she cried, her eyes shining into his. "I've never been so happy in my life."

"You do?" A strange little smiled tugged at the corners of his mouth, and again he looked decidedly pleased. "Well, that's fine."

Andie laughed happily. *"Fine?* Is that all you can say? Fine?" She linked her arm through his, snuggling close to him. "Come on, honey. I've got some big plans for the rest of this evening."

"Oh? I hope they include me."

She stood on her toes and kissed him on the nose. "You're the guest of honor. Now, we'll begin with a round of outrageously good champagne at that restaurant with the garden. Goodness, I'm so frazzled I don't think I could eat a bite, but if you're hungry, we'll have dinner— that is, if you want to." She giggled again, dizzy with excitement, and kissed him once more. "And after dinner, we'll go back to my place and spend the rest of the night making mad, passionate love." She looked up at him, her green eyes sparkling. "Now, how does that sound?"

His arm went around her, pulling her close. "That sounds great—especially that last part."

"Good."

Andie wasn't used to drinking, and the champagne went straight to her head. After two glasses, she was floating pleasantly on a sea of unparalleled delight. Giddy with happiness, she took George's hand in hers and held it intimately throughout the evening. She chattered effortlessly, telling George every little bit of news that had happened while he was away, and sharing her innermost thoughts with him.

As they strolled home in the cool night, she leaned against him and let out a shaky sigh. George hadn't said very much all evening, but perhaps that had been her fault. A tiny little voice told her that something was bothering him, but she dismissed that as ridiculous. She brushed it aside and concentrated on drawing him out.

"Good grief, George," she said abruptly, "I've been doing all the talking, haven't I? Well, I guess I haven't let you get a word in edgewise. It must be the champagne. Champagne does that to me. It just gets me going like a nonstop engine. In fact—" She stopped, slapping a hand across her mouth. "Oh, no, there I go again. You'll have to shut me up, George." Giving him a sly wink, she added, "And I know just the method to use."

"What's that?" he asked with a sly grin. His lambent eyes were hooded.

"Come up to my lair and I'll show you."

They ran up the steps hand in hand, their hearts pounding. Inside Andie's apartment, they fell immediately into each other's arms, trading long, luxurious kisses and letting their hands roam freely. Andie was lost in contentment as she surrendered herself to him, wanting him to know and command every part of her body. His fingers plied the buttons on the front of her dress deftly, opening them hungrily to reveal her pert, upright breasts, already ripe with anticipation.

She arched her back slightly to offer him her breasts more fully, and he bent to take them into his mouth, one by one. His persuasive caresses produced soft moans of pleasure from her. She stepped back and slid the dress down her legs, stepping out of it so that she was nearly naked before him. George wasted no time in pursuing her, stepping forward to kiss her breasts again, and then moving down to kiss the soft mound of her belly and the sensitive insides of her thighs. When she was gasping with need, he hooked his hands over the sides of her while lace bikini panties and pulled them down.

Andie closed her eyes and muttered incoherent words of pure pleasure as he tasted her, sending her into a sweet, dreamy world that only he could create for her. When her knees became too weak to hold her, he lifted her up and carried her to the bed.

She watched as he stood over her, swiftly unbuttoning his shirt and throwing it to one side. His bare bronzed chest seemed to glow in the dim light, inviting her to touch it. She did, reveling in the smoothness of skin over the unyielding hardness of muscle. "Oh, George," she whispered as she watched his eyes close in passion. "To think that we'll be able to do this every night for the rest of our lives."

"Every night . . . and every day," he agreed, shedding the rest of his clothes and joining her on the bed. He looked at her face, stopping her with the piercing strength of his gaze. Andie shivered, stunned by the passion she saw in his eyes. They were a brazen amber in the darkness, raking her body with an almost physical force. "Andie," he whispered, thrilling her to the core. "You do want this? You want to share your life with me, no matter what?"

She nodded, too shaken to speak. At that moment, she loved him so much that she felt her heart would overflow. But something occurred to her. "Not just you," she whispered earnestly. "Speedy, too."

His eyes seemed to settle then, quieting as he took her in his arms. Her head turned, resting on his shoulder. That must have been what was bothering him, she thought. There was nothing to worry about now. Everything was going to be wonderful. The tiny kernel of doubt faded into the back of her mind.

They kissed again, gliding together and sealing their passion with tender exchanges. As they rose and fell together, spiraling toward a summit of passion, Andie clung to George with all her might, wanting the symbol of this night to last forever.

But when the magic was over, when she lay peacefully in his arms, caught in the first tendrils of sleep, the tiny shred of doubt crept forward, intruding into what should have been a perfect moment. It rose before her, full blown, presenting her with a sudden, dark revelation. She had offered her body and soul to George, and had proclaimed her love.

Lying there in the dark, she realized what was missing. George had never said he loved her, too.

Chapter Eleven

"CONGRATULATIONS."

Andie blinked as she recognized Morty Carlson's nasal voice on her office phone. "For what?" she asked.

"I hear you're getting married," he answered. "George told me all about it yesterday afternoon. I just finished drawing up the final adoption papers."

Andie was totally bewildered. "Adoption papers? Yesterday?"

"Yes," Morty answered crisply. "Why? Is there anything the matter?"

She thought quickly, stalling for time. "I-I'm not sure."

There was a strange silence. Then Morty continued cautiously, "You *are* getting married, aren't you?"

"Uh—yes, but how did you find out about it before me?" she stammered. "George only proposed last night."

There was complete silence on both ends as they each deduced what had happened. No wonder George had seemed so sly and secretive last night! His whole proposal had been part of his scheme to keep Speedy. She was apparently nothing more than a convenient stand-in for a much-needed role.

"I've been had," Andie whispered to herself, stunned.

Morty cleared his throat and covered smoothly. "Well, ah, I'm sure it's all for the best. From what I can see, you and George will make a very fine couple. And now that you have a son to add to your lives, you'll be blessed with even more happiness."

Andie was barely listening. "What did I get myself into?" she whispered. Her hand and her head dropped forward onto the desk.

"Oh, Ms. Maguire? Are you still there?"

"Yes—I—uh, I'll call you back." She hung up without waiting for a response.

She didn't want to see anyone at that moment, but Lou came bursting in, obviously all business.

"Hey, Maguire! I liked that idea you came up with at the meeting yesterday."

Andie looked up at her boss with dazed eyes.

"Oh, no," Collier muttered. "He's at it again, huh?" He waved his hand at her dismissively. "This time I really don't want to hear about it. Your personal problems are just that—personal."

"What's personal?" Gail asked with lively interest as she poked her head through the open door. "Hi, Andie."

Andie didn't answer, didn't move.

"Hey, Andie!" Gail said. She came in and waved a hand over her face. "Earth to Andie, earth to Andie." She looked at Collier. "What's the matter with her?"

"I'll tell you what's the matter," Lou answered irritably. "She's in love—with a maniac. Am I right? Hey! Maguire?"

Andie wasn't listening. "I can't believe George would do that," she muttered. "I just can't believe it."

Gail shook her head. "Uh-oh, this sounds serious."

"Yeah, like a well-worn soap opera," Collier said dryly. But he stopped when Gail threw him a stern look.

"Talk to me, kid," Gail encouraged. "What happened?"

"I'm getting married," Andie said.

"Hey, congratulations," Lou said, surprised. "You had me worried there for a second."

"To a devious, lying skunk," she added as her face fell in dismay.

"I knew I should have knocked before entering," Lou said. He started to get up, but Gail stopped him.

"Stick around, Lou," Gail ordered. "We may need your opinion on this. You seem to know as much about George as I do."

Collier signed and perched on Andie's desk. "Okay," he relented. "Let's hear the latest development."

The explanation was brief. Lou and Gail already knew the bare facts, and they listened eagerly as Andie filled them in on the rest. When the tale was over, Gail had only one suggestion.

"Marry him."

Andie looked up, truly surprised. "What?"

"You heard me. Get married."

"But *why?*"

"Because you love him, that's why, dummy."

Andie's eyes filled with tears. "But he doesn't love me."

"How do you know that?" Gail pressed. "Did he say he doesn't love you?"

"Well, no, but he didn't say he does. Doesn't it seem like a logical, reasonable thing to say to somebody you're proposing to? I mean, it's not exactly a minor detail."

"Maybe it is to him," Lou put in.

"That's right," Gail agreed. "You're expecting too much from him. After all, he's not that experienced."

"What do you mean?" Andie countered defensively. She couldn't imagine why she felt the need to stick up for George, but she did. "He's not a babe in the woods, you know. He's been around."

Gail sighed wearily. "Andie, Andie," she admonished, shaking her head. "Don't you know anything? George is just shy, that's all."

This was too much. *"George? Shy?"* She let out a cynical snort. "You've got to be kidding."

Gail took the other corner of the desk and leaned forward, commanding Andie's attention. "Now, you listen to me. I know he's a sophisticated man. I know he's had other relationships. But he's still a man, and most men are deficient in certain important areas."

Lou cocked an eyebrow and looked at her suspiciously. "Oh, yeah? What's that?"

"It's very basic." Gail shrugged. "Most men need a little training, that's all." Andie couldn't help smiling, and even Lou listened, interested in spite of himself, as Gail drove her point home. "George is very good at what he does, right?" Andie nodded. "And he's suave and gorgeous and he swept you off your feet, right?" Another nod. "But that's just the point. George has spent most of his life being an achiever, striving to fit a certain male image that he's created in his mind. So he's very good at achieving and at coming across the way he thinks he should. All of that is very attractive—but it doesn't include a very crucial area."

Andie nodded again, slowly this time. "I think I see what you mean."

Lou almost exploded. "Well, I don't! What are you two dames getting at, anyway?"

"It's very simple," Andie said earnestly, eyeing Gail with new respect. "George didn't tell me how he felt because it didn't occur to him. After all, if he was really planning on deceiving me, he would have made sure to declare his undying love just to get me to say yes."

"Very true." Gail nodded. "Good point."

"Still," Andie worried, "he's a very clever man. I guess I'll just have to work on him." The thought that George was really that conniving made her heart lurch. "God, Gail, I hope you're right."

Lou looked from one woman to the other. "Is that it? Are you two finished analyzing?"

The phone rang.

"Hello, Ms. Maguire?" It was Morty Carlson and he sounded terse and more humorless than ever.

"Uh, yes?"

"Can you be at Mr. Demarest's apartment at five o'-clock sharp?" he asked, almost ordering.

"Yes, but what is it? Is anything wrong?"

"Something's come up regarding little Joshua. I'm afraid it may put a damper on your plans."

He refused to give her any details. Andie wrote down the time and hung up distractedly.

Lou simply smiled as if he somehow knew what was to come. "As we say in the daytime-drama biz—the plot thickens."

At five o'clock sharp, Andie sat uncomfortably next to George, waiting with bated breath as Morty placed several forms on the coffee table in front of them. Speedy sat on the floor nearby, playing with a bunch of toys, while George sat stiffly, his hands nervously gripping the sides of his chair.

"I'm afraid I have bad news for both of you," Morty announced. "It seems Mindy has changed her mind. She refuses to sign the release papers. She had decided to keep Joshua after all."

George's face dropped and Andie gasped audibly. "I don't believe it!" he shouted. He stood up and leaned forward, looking over the papers as if there were something he needed to see. "I spent a whole week working this out with her, and she assured me that if I didn't adopt Speedy, she would put him up for adoption herself."

"I'm sorry," Morty said. He held up one of the papers. "She signed this form demanding that Joshua be taken to California immediately. She has decided to exercise her rights as the natural mother."

It was as if a bomb had been set off in George's living room. George turned beet red, rage and acute disappointment warring on his face. Andie couldn't hold back her tears, knowing that her sorrow was for all three of them, for the real family they had yearned to become. She looked at George's bereft face helplessly, wanting to comfort him but not knowing how or where to begin.

"Oh, George!" she cried. "I'm so sorry."

He put his arm around her and tried to console her. "It's all right. Maybe Mindy has shaped up. Maybe— maybe Speedy will be better off. Isn't that right, Morty?" he asked desperately.

Morty didn't say a word.

"I can't believe it," Andie moaned, letting her tears fall on her dress. "I'll miss him so much."

George's voice was strangely controlled, as if he were trying not to cry himself. "We can have children of our own."

"We can?" she sobbed. Then she looked up at him in

surprise. "You mean you still want to marry me? Even if you can't have Speedy?"

It was George's turn to be surprised. "What do you mean? Of course I want to marry you. What does Speedy have to do with that?"

Andie hesitated, reluctant to say everything in front of Morty, the professional busybody. But she reasoned that he already knew everything she was about to say anyway. Besides, this was no time for propriety. There was too much at stake. "I—I thought you only wanted to marry me so they would let you keep Speedy," she confessed. "Morty told me this morning that you had already announced our engagement yesterday afternoon."

George looked astonished. He turned to Morty with a gesture of pure outrage. "Do you believe this?"

"Quite frankly," Morty answered, "yes, I do. I have to admit, it all sounded quite calculated to me." He favored them with a thin smile. "But now I'm not so sure." He looked shrewdly at George and asked him point-blank, "Do you love this woman?"

George looked shocked, but he swallowed hard and turned to Andie, capturing her eyes before answering. "Yes, I do," he said quietly. "I love her very much."

Andie melted into a thousand pieces. She took his face in her hands and kissed him slowly and sweetly.

"Congratulations," Morty said. "I now pronounce you a family." He wrote something briskly on one of his numerous forms, chuckling and smugly content. Andie and George stared in utter bewilderment. "It's all final," Morty added with a grin. "On the day of your wedding, you'll be more than just husband and wife—you'll also be father and mother as well."

No one spoke. The silence was electric with tension.

"I lied," Morty admitted cheerfully. "Mindy doesn't want Speedy. She wants you two to adopt him." He handed George a form. "See, that's her signature at the bottom, notorized by the courts. It's all quite legal."

"But why the ruse?" George demanded.

"I could ask you the same question, Mr. Demarest," Morty countered sternly. "You told me Andie had already agreed to marry you. But she hadn't even been asked!"

George nodded. "Okay, so I jumped the gun a little. Call it wishful thinking. I just knew she had to say yes. It was all I could think about. Maybe I was a little hasty— but I was right in predicting her answer, wasn't I?" He looked boyishly proud, and Andie giggled.

"Yes, you were absolutely right," she said, patting him on the arm.

Suddenly, she felt a small hand tugging at her dress. Looking down into Speedy's earnest round face, she smiled through her tears of relief. "What is it, honey?"

"I hungwy!" Speedy informed them. "I want choc-vit!"

George reached promptly into his pocket and produced a miniature bite-size Hershey bar. "Here you go," he said, lifting Speedy onto his lap and resting his cheek against the little boy's tousled hair. He closed his eyes for a moment, and there was a sweet, poignant silence as Andie watched him, love brimming in her eyes.

"Well, I must say, you're certainly prepared," Morty observed after a moment.

"Of course," Andie said, beaming at her new family. "He's very efficient, you know."

SECOND CHANCE AT LOVE

COMING NEXT MONTH

SWANN'S SONG #334 by Carole Buck
Knowing both karate and kids, Megan Harper poses
as a nanny to secretly guard rock star Colin Swann and
his irrepressible son...and gets into deep
trouble when love complicates the deception!

STOLEN KISSES #335 by Liz Grady
Mattie Hamilton is rehearsing a museum
heist when tuxedo-clad thief Devlin Seamus Devlin
tackles her in midair...and offers to tutor
her in *all* kinds of midnight maneuvers!

GOLDEN GIRL #336 by Jacqueline Topaz
In sophisticated Hollywood, schoolteacher Olivia Gold
finds both her movie star grandmother *and* dashing soulmate
Andrew Carr—who transforms her into a glittering
golden girl and spellbinds her with sensual enchantment.

SMILES OF A SUMMER NIGHT #337 by Delaney Devers
Like a modern rogue, plantation owner
Jules Robichaux sweeps April Jasper away with cynical
charm, smoothly seduces her under moonlit
magnolias...but won't trust her enough to offer his love.

DESTINY'S DARLING #338 by Adrienne Edwards
"Bought" by ex-husband Bart Easton at a charity
benefit, Dot Biancardi recalls poignant moments—of
gallant courtship, wedded bliss...and lonely
heartache. Dare she risk repeating past mistakes?

WILD AND WONDERFUL #339 by Lee Williams
Trapped on a wild Maine island with brawny recluse
Greg Bowles, who's rejected the inheritance she's come to
give him, heir hunter Alicia Saunders finds a new
tension building...desire quickening.

SECOND CHANCE AT LOVE

Be Sure to Read These New Releases!

BELONGING TO TAYLOR #322 by Kay Robbins
Taylor Shannon employs her mindreading
talents, psychic family, peculiar pets, and sexy
satins to lure gallant but reluctant Trevor
King, then pursues him until he catches her!

ANYWHERE AND ALWAYS #323 by Lee Williams
Brilliant inventor Justin Fuller, an Albert
Einstein and offbeat Romeo in one explosively sensual
package, dazzles Lydie Henley with high-tech
wizardry and X-rated kisses...but makes no promises.

FORTUNE'S CHOICE #324 by Elissa Curry
Destitute socialite "Joey" Fortune
and dashing ne'er-do-well Nick Parmenter join
forces to recoup their losses by selling ice
cream...and discover sweet love.

LADY ON THE LINE #325 by Cait Logan
Arrogantly chauvinistic one moment, hot and
tender the next, Barrett Redding is almost more man than
K.C. Bollins can handle—especially when his underlying
vulnerability threatens to crush her last resistance!

A KISS AWAY #326 by Sherryl Woods
With her fortieth birthday approaching, Jessica
Warren tries—but fails—to resist erotically roguish Kevin
Lawrence, whose playfulness and gleaming pectorals
utterly undermine her sense of what's proper...

PLAY IT AGAIN, SAM #327 by Petra Diamond
When brash Hollywood designer Sam
Harrison invades nostalgic Nedda Shaw's sleepy
Southern town, she's too bollixed to
distinguish between a summer fling and lasting love.

Order on opposite page

SECOND CHANCE AT LOVE

___ 0-425-08627-5	SPRING MADNESS #299 Aimée Duvall	$2.25
___ 0-425-08628-3	SIREN'S SONG #300 Linda Barlow	$2.25
___ 0-425-08629-1	MAN OF HER DREAMS #301 Katherine Granger	$2.25
___ 0-425-08630-5	UNSPOKEN LONGINGS #302 Dana Daniels	$2.25
___ 0-425-08631-3	THIS SHINING HOUR #303 Antonia Tyler	$2.25
___ 0-425-08672-0	THE FIRE WITHIN #304 Laine Allen	$2.25
___ 0-425-08673-9	WHISPERS OF AN AUTUMN DAY #305 Lee Williams	$2.25
___ 0-425-08674-7	SHADY LADY #306 Jan Mathews	$2.25
___ 0-425-08675-5	TENDER IS THE NIGHT #307 Helen Carter	$2.25
___ 0-425-08676-3	FOR LOVE OF MIKE #308 Courtney Ryan	$2.25
___ 0-425-08677-1	TWO IN A HUDDLE #309 Diana Morgan	$2.25
___ 0-425-08749-1	LOVERS AND PRETENDERS #310 Liz Grady	$2.25
___ 0-425-08750-6	SWEETS TO THE SWEET #311 Jeanne Grant	$2.25
___ 0-425-08751-4	EVER SINCE EVE #312 Kasey Adams	$2.25
___ 0-425-08752-2	BLITHE SPIRIT #313 Mary Haskell	$2.25
___ 0-425-08753-0	MAN AROUND THE HOUSE #314 Joan Darling	$2.25
___ 0-425-08754-9	DRIVEN TO DISTRACTION #315 Jamisan Whitney	$2.25
___ 0-425-08850-2	DARK LIGHTNING #316 Karen Keast	$2.25
___ 0-425-08851-0	MR. OCTOBER #317 Carole Buck	$2.25
___ 0-425-08852-9	ONE STEP TO PARADISE #318 Jasmine Craig	$2.25
___ 0-425-08853-7	TEMPTING PATIENCE #319 Christina Dair	$2.25
___ 0-425-08854-5	ALMOST LIKE BEING IN LOVE #320 Betsy Osborne	$2.25
___ 0-425-08855-3	ON CLOUD NINE #321 Jean Kent	$2.25
___ 0-425-08908-8	BELONGING TO TAYLOR #322 Kay Robbins	$2.25
___ 0-425-08909-6	ANYWHERE AND ALWAYS #323 Lee Williams	$2.25
___ 0-425-08910-X	FORTUNE'S CHOICE #324 Elissa Curry	$2.25
___ 0-425-08911-8	LADY ON THE LINE #325 Cait Logan	$2.25
___ 0-425-08948-7	A KISS AWAY #326 Sherryl Woods	$2.25
___ 0-425-08949-5	PLAY IT AGAIN, SAM #327 Petra Diamond	$2.25
___ 0-425-08966-5	SNOWFLAME #328 Christa Merlin	$2.25
___ 0-425-08967-3	BRINGING UP BABY #329 Diana Morgan	$2.25
___ 0-425-08968-1	DILLON'S PROMISE #330 Cinda Richards	$2.25
___ 0-425-08969-X	BE MINE, VALENTINE #331 Hilary Cole	$2.25
___ 0-425-08970-3	SOUTHERN COMFORT #332 Kit Windham	$2.25
___ 0-425-08971-1	NO PLACE FOR A LADY #333 Cassie Miles	$2.25

Available at your local bookstore or return this form to:

SECOND CHANCE AT LOVE
THE BERKLEY PUBLISHING GROUP, Dept. B
390 Murray Hill Parkway, East Rutherford, NJ 07073

Please send me the titles checked above. I enclose _____. Include $1.00 for postage and handling if one book is ordered; 25¢ per book for two or more not to exceed $1.75. New York residents please add sales tax. Prices are subject to change without notice and may be higher in Canada.

NAME_____

ADDRESS_____

CITY_____STATE/ZIP_____

(Allow six weeks for delivery.)   SK-41b

A STIRRING PAGEANTRY
OF
HISTORICAL ROMANCE

Shana Carrol

___ 0-515-08249-X Rebels in Love $3.95

Roberta Gellis

___ 0-515-08230-9 Bond of Blood $3.95

___ 0-515-07529-9 Fire Song $3.95

___ 0-515-08600-2 A Tapestry of Dreams $3.95

Jill Gregory

___ 0-515-07100-5 The Wayward Heart $3.50

___ 0-515-07728-3 To Distant Shores $3.50

___ 0-425-07666-0 My True and Tender Love $6.95
(A Berkley Trade Paperback)

___ 0-515-08585-5 Moonlit Obsession $6.95
(A Jove Trade Paperback)

___ 0-515-08389-5 Promise Me The Dawn $3.95

Mary Pershall

___ 0-425-07020-4 A Shield of Roses $3.95

Francine Rivers

___ 0-515-08181-7 Sycamore Hill $3.50

___ 0-515-06823-3 This Golden Valley $3.50

Pamela Belle

___ 0-425-08268-7 The Moon in the Water $3.95

___ 0-425-07367-X The Chains of Fate $6.95
(A Berkley Trade Paperback)
